MW01178059

JAGDISH R.

PANDORA'S HEARTACHES

PublishAmerica
Baltimore

© 2005 by Jagdish R. Singh.
All rights reserved. No part of this book may be reproduced, stored in a retrieval system or transmitted in any form or by any means without the prior written permission of the publishers, except by a reviewer who may quote brief passages in a review to be printed in a newspaper, magazine or journal.

First printing

At the specific preference of the author, Publish America allowed this work to remain exactly as the author intended, verbatim, without editorial input.

ISBN: 1-4241-0144-1
PUBLISHED BY PUBLISHAMERICA, LLLP
www.publishamerica.com
Baltimore

Printed in the United States of America

Preface

"Pandora's Heartaches" is a collection of fictional stories that are based on contemporary issues, depicting themes of infidelity, sexual preferences, insubordination, adversity, marriage, acts of terror, human behavior, hunger, celibacy and spiritual beliefs. These topics are carefully woven into each story, enabling readers to analyze many of their earthly disparities and diverse beliefs.

Contents

An Afterlife Dream

It was nightfall when my close relatives and friends arrived at the Rosewood Funeral Home to view my dead body and to pay their final respects. As they all gathered around my coffin which was fully open, some of them began to weep in sorrow. Though my physical body was dead, I was very much alive in thought for I could see them lamenting over my dead body. Being aloft and constantly hovering around them, I desperately tried to tell everyone not to grieve. However, since I was invisible, it was impossible for them to see me.

I was ninety–four years of age when I passed away and was greatly relieved to do so, for I had been suffering too long in the later years of my life. Looking back at the period of suffering I had endured, I must say that the most distraught period in my life was when my eldest daughter had me put into a home for seniors when I reached age eighty. Though I was greatly disappointed when she did this, I did not harbor any ill feelings for her, but was thankful that she took good care of me amid her duties as a married woman with three children. I realized that as she grew older it became too burdensome for her to keep up with the additional responsibility of taking care of me. The years I had spent in the home for seniors were for the greater part a sad experience, for there was little for me to enjoy being old, sickly and lonely. In anguish I prayed each day to die, for I had grown tired of nurses treating me like an infant and doctors giving me various medicines to keep me alive. With life appearing meaningless to me, I could not understand why they had denied me the right to die, for my prolonged suffering had seriously tormented my mind.

Here at the Rosewood Funeral Home, I was very disappointed listening to the speeches of some of my grandchildren who were emphasizing how much they were going to miss me. Sadly, after I was put into the seniors home, only two of them came to visit me, but here at my funeral, I felt annoyed listening to the others talk about what a loving and kind person I was.

Later that night, I heard the priest who had been chosen to perform my final rites announcing that it was time for everyone to leave the funeral home, and that I would be buried at 10:00 a.m the following day. I became deeply saddened, knowing that I would be left alone, and also worrying about what would become of me after my physical body was buried.

After everyone had left, my coffin was moved into another room by two men who quickly closed it, then shut the door and left. With the lights now turned off, the room appeared dark and deserted. In this lonely place I began to hover around my body. While doing so, I heard the crying voice of a young boy in the same room, grieving at the loss of his physical body. I became deeply touched and pleaded with him not to cry, because his grieving was making me more distressed. Fortunately, he instantly stopped and then quietly told me that his name was Peter and that he had died in an accident two days ago. Peter claimed that life was unfair, for he wasn't allowed to become an adult because of his sudden death. He sorrowfully emphasized how much he missed his parents who were stricken with grief.

During our quiet talk in the wee hours of the night, I mentioned to Peter that I was ninety–four years of age when I died, and he told me how happy he would have felt if he were granted such a long life. However, when I recounted how much suffering I had endured when I became old, he became very concerned and politely asked me if there was anything he could do to come back to life. As I began considering how to answer, a beautiful young lady suddenly opened the door and began pushing my coffin out of the room and into another which was beautifully decorated with flowers.

From the windows in this room I could tell it was the break of dawn, as I could see the sun slowly rising. When this charming lady opened a box containing cosmetics, I realized that she was a mortician. As she gently combed my hair and put make-up on my face, I began to secretly admire her and in so doing my feelings began to change. Though I could not feel her gentle touch, the affectionate manner in which she was treating my body made me fall in love with her. My thoughts became filled with desire and my love for this mortician became stronger. Knowing that there were only a few hours remaining before my physical body would be buried, I began expressing my love for her, but unfortunately, she could not hear or see me because I was invisible. I began to lament, thinking that it all seemed unfair, for here I was feeling youthful, yet this beautiful lady I adored could not see or talk to me.

A short while later, she moved me into a huge room in preparation for people to view my body. She opened my coffin and then quietly left. It suddenly dawned on me that my body would soon be buried, and this might be the last time I would ever see my loved ones.

Finally, the moment came for my body to be concealed, and here at the burial site I heard one of my relatives talk about how greatly I would be missed. It was a sad moment for everyone as I watched helplessly from above many of my close relatives weeping in sorrow.

After the short homily, my coffin was gently lowered into a

hole. As I watched in great sadness at my coffin being covered with clay, I began to think what would become of me when everyone left this burial site. Within minutes, a mysterious voice suddenly cried out, "You are no longer attached to your physical body and everything you see, hear and do are from now on an illusion. You are now free to dwell anywhere or create with your thoughts anything you desire."

Hearing that it was all an illusion was not entirely pleasing, but being given the chance to choose, the thought of God came to me. When alive I had always wished to dwell with God in everlasting peace after I die, and here it seemed that I now had the opportunity to do so. However, after deliberating for sometime on how much happiness I would find dwelling with God, I decided not to choose the Lord as my everlasting companion. Though I loved God dearly, my desire to dwell with a fellow human being was greater.

Thinking deeply about the mortal being I loved the most, the thought of my wife came to mind. But since she had died at age eighty, I wondered how much joy I would find living with my wife who was probably still old and sickly. Though I felt that this was unfair, I strongly believed that it would be better to follow my heartfelt feelings. Reflecting further, the thought of dwelling with the mortician whom I was so madly in love with suddenly came to mind, and I became filled with desire to have her as my everlasting companion. Without hesitation, I cried out loud that she was the one I would like to dwell with forever. The mysterious voice replied, "Your wish has been granted and you are now free to fabricate your own heaven and dwell in it with the one you care to be with the most."

Though it is all a figment of my imagination, I am pleased with the choice I've made since it comforts me. Although it seems like a selfish one, it appears that having such a desire lends continuity in afterlife. Now that I feel liberated, I am drawn to think that a desire of some kind is what sustains one's thoughts or true self after the demise of their physical body.

Now that I exist as pure consciousness, I've realized that heaven and hell, as my loved ones on Earth perceive it to be, does not exist. In short, I can create my own. Because my emotions and desires remain very much the same as on Earth, I realize that if I cannot control them, I could easily create my own hell by agonizing over earthly things. Fortunately, in the later stage of my life on Earth, I took some time to seek the discipline of understanding and to maintain my belief in fairness. This was rewarding, for these righteous thoughts helped me to create my own heavenly abode of peace and bliss.

Lessons of Marriage

Soma Badani was from a tender age moody and hard to please. Being the only child of a wealthy and highly respected family, she was adored and pampered by her parents. However, amid all the affection, her parents were very concerned about her ill–mannered behavior, which seemed to get worse as she grew older.

When Soma reached age twenty, her parents suggested that she be married, believing it would improve her decorum and make her act more responsibly. However, Soma was so temperamental that she immediately made it clear that she would not marry until she completed a university degree in business administration. Her parents, seeing how agitated she was, refrained from coercing her, and instead, they agreed to let her complete her studies.

* * *

Four years later, Soma graduated and during a social party to celebrate her success, she was introduced by her parents to a handsome man named Gupta whom her father held in high esteem. From this introduction, Soma and Gupta found a lot in common to talk about, leading many to think that they were well-suited.

Later that evening, the parents of both observed their lengthy conversation and felt that Soma and Gupta would make a perfect couple if they were to get married. Since they were very interested in making a match, without hesitation, they approached Soma and Gupta to ask if they would consider marrying each other. Though Soma and Gupta were very surprised by what they were asked, they did not reject the idea, but politely requested that they see each other more often before making a commitment. With their parents' blessings, they were allowed to meet each other, making way for a period of courtship.

In the following months, Soma discovered Gupta to be polite and well-mannered as her father had claimed. His kind disposition won her heart and a month later, of her own accord, she agreed to marry Gupta. Her father Govinda was absolutely delighted when he heard this, thinking that with Gupta's noble qualities, he would be the ideal person to marry his temperamental daughter.

After months of preparation, the day for the wedding finally came, and both bride and groom looked admirable in their traditional wedding costumes. As they glanced at each other during the wedding ceremony, their hearts seemed to ignite with love as the desire to be with each other appeared strong. Their wedding turned out to be joyous and pleasing to all, leading the guests to believe that this couple would be united in matrimony for decades to come.

After the wedding, Soma and Gupta moved into a brand new home which Govinda had bought for the newly married couple. He was a wealthy man who wanted to see his daughter dwell in comfort and not have to worry about the expenses of owning a home. In the first couple of months, they proved to be compatible, having a great deal to talk and laugh about. Gupta turned out to be a fine gentleman as her parents had said. Whatever Soma desired or wanted him to do, he tried his utmost to please her. Since he was soft-spoken and very attentive to his wife, Soma became the more assertive one, and with time, she began to make most of the decisions for her husband as to his household duties, the way he dressed and what he should or should not do.

Continuing to play the dominant role, Soma soon wanted to have everything done her way. Though Gupta was a little displeased with his wife's bossy attitude, he always tried to avoid a confrontation with her. In months to follow, Soma became less attentive to her husband and slowly her affection for him diminished. Eventually, it got to the point where she seldom spoke to Gupta and no longer wished to be with him.

Finally, after fourteen months of marriage, Soma approached her husband asking that they be divorced because she no longer loved him. This greatly disturbed Gupta, since he considered marriage a sacred thing, and could never imagine his wife and himself becoming separated so easily. From then on, he lamented each day over what wrong he might have done to cause his wife to dislike him.

Gupta tried to get his wife to change her mind, pleading with her not to leave, fearing that the news would certainly make their parents distraught. Soma, however, had made up her mind, claiming that she had lost any loving feelings for her husband and would be returning to university to further her studies. Gupta, hearing that his wife no longer loved him, felt it was useless to continue their relationship, so he consented to give her a divorce.

The news was a stunning surprise to all their parents, who had been close friends for many years. Govinda still wanted to maintain his friendship with Gupta's parents, so he told them that their son was a noble person who should not be blamed for anything. Instead, he accused his daughter of being inconsiderate and solely responsible for ruining the marriage.

* * *

Two years later, Soma met and fell in love with a man named Carl Peterson who was ten years older than her. Like her first husband Gupta, Carl treated her well. But he was not over-pleasing like Gupta, since he was not willing to do everything his wife wished.

After she married Carl, Soma discovered that he was an upright person who did not have much in common with her, for he had different religious beliefs, liked different foods and was an ardent sports fan. Since her first marriage was abortive, she decided to take a different approach to make her marriage to Carl one of happiness. She began to adopt most of the things Carl liked such as dressing to please him, eating the foods he chose, and even joining his faith.

During this marriage, Govinda came only once to her home, and was very disappointed when he saw how willing Soma was to serve Carl whatever he wanted to eat or drink. Her father was drawn to think that she succumbed easier to Carl than Gupta, for he remembered once when Gupta had politely asked her to make him a cup of tea that she flatly refused, telling him to get it himself. Knowing that her parents were very angry with her for divorcing Gupta, Soma chose not to keep close ties with them, fearing they would say negative things about Carl.

Apart from the minor fall-outs with her parents, Soma's relationship with Carl was a good one for she seemed happy and rarely showed any signs of being moody. Unfortunately, however, this marriage only lasted two years. One day Carl gave Soma a stunning surprise by stating that he wished to divorce her. Carl said that he had been dating another woman for over six months, and would be moving out to live with her. When Soma heard this, she became very confused and hurriedly telephoned her father to tell him what Carl had said. In anguish, she pleaded with Govinda to advise her what to do, but he was rude and told her to solve her own problems.

After months of living apart, Soma and Carl got divorced and she was now living alone. Having been divorced twice, she vowed never to get married again. This was a worrisome period for Soma, and she began thinking of ways to avoid falling into a state of depression. Reflecting on her studies in business administration and her current financial status, it suddenly dawned on her to become an entrepreneur. Soma sold the luxurious home her father had bought for her and Gupta, and opened a jewelry shop, believing that such a business would yield huge profits.

It was at this store that she met and later fell in love with a customer named Jerome. Like Gupta and Carl, Jerome impressed her a great deal for he appeared to be a caring person. However, having passed through two broken marriages, her relationship with Jerome was different. She was truthful about past marriages, and he was very sympathetic. After meaningful discussions about the type of relationship they would have, they both agreed to live together in her apartment but never to get married.

Now that Soma was living with Jerome, she learnt for the first time that he was unemployed and had been looking for work over a year. Earlier, Jerome had mentioned to her that he was an accountant, so she did not question him but assumed that he was employed. Jerome, believing that this might be a serious concern to Soma, told her not to worry, and made a promise that as soon as he found a job, he would assist her financially. Surprisingly, Soma was not overly concerned for judging from Jerome's caring demeanor, she seemed confident that he would keep his promise.

During the period Jerome was unemployed, Soma assisted him financially. And it appeared to her that he was a generous man, for whatever money she gave him, he always took a portion of it to buy her a nice gift. With Jerome seemingly kind to her, she trusted him a great deal and began to share many of her personal secrets with him. It was from this trust that Jerome found out that she had over seven hundred thousand dollars in the bank.

* * *

Six months later, Soma learned from her doctor that she was pregnant, and at this stage of her life a child was most welcome. When Jerome heard of her pregnancy he was very excited, and began talking about a promising future for the two of them with the coming of their child. He instantly proposed marriage to Soma, but she politely refused after thinking about her two previous marriages. A few days later while rethinking matters, it suddenly dawned on Soma that if she did not marry Jerome, she would bear a child out of wedlock. Not wanting this to happen and very much concerned about what people might say, she broke her vow and consented to get married to Jerome.

Their wedding was a private one, and sadly, only one month after they were married, Soma had a miscarriage and lost her baby. While she was deeply saddened, Jerome, on the other hand, appeared less worried. With Soma's pregnancy terminated, Jerome soon revealed a darker side, for his intentions were now to live mainly off her earnings. Being her lawful husband, he seemed confident that she would give him all the financial support he needed.

In the following months, Jerome proved to be lazy for he made no effort to find a job, and was quite content to live mainly off Soma's earnings. Soma now deeply regretted marrying Jerome, since her only reason for doing so was not to have a child out of wedlock. Soon, they were having frequent quarrels and harsh words for each other. Whenever Soma encouraged Jerome to find a job, he became very angry and would spend a night or two away from home. This turned out to be worrisome for Soma, for whenever she confronted him for not coming home, he became argumentative and threatened to hurt her. Since Soma had had two broken marriages, she felt that she had no other choice but to remain married to Jerome in spite of his hostile behavior. She came to think that a third divorce would certainly make people think that she was a difficult person to get along with.

Soon, Jerome began to physically abuse Soma, thinking that if he divorced her, he would be legally entitled to a portion of her money. As Soma reflected on Jerome's behavior, she concluded that she had been deceived by a pretentious man who was only interested in her wealth.

Soma's marriage to Jerome lasted another two years until it had gotten to the point where she honestly felt that Jerome might kill her out of anger. In the divorce settlement, Jerome was awarded one-fifth of her savings and he was absolutely delighted with the amount of money he got from divorcing her. But Soma deeply regretted not signing a prenuptial agreement, since she honestly felt that he never contributed anything towards their marriage. It seemed that she had placed too much trust in him and never knew what his real intentions were.

A distraught Soma, now living alone again, began to reflect

on her past marriages, and now she deeply regretted renouncing her marriage with Gupta. It was only when she was treated unfairly by Carl and Jerome that she came to appreciate Gupta's loyalty to her. Soma would hereafter spend many years pondering why she had treated the humble Gupta with so much disrespect while adoring Carl who was less polite and more demanding. In analyzing it all, she was drawn to think that her domineering attitude had forced Gupta to be timorous, fearing a confrontation with her might ruin their marriage. However, with Carl and Jerome the circumstances were different: to sustain a peaceful relationship and make her marriage last, she not only had to succumb to whatever they asked for, but had to change her overassertive attitude. Looking back, she blamed herself for taking advantage of Gupta's humbleness. And sadly, her two other broken marriages greatly affected her, making her feel not only cheated, but also that something was wrong with her.

The Fragility of Life

Romel Wilson was a retired member of parliament who spent most of his leisure time visiting the major attractions of various nations. At age fifty-five he was still unmarried and very reserved, for he seldom met or communicated with his relatives. Having no serious commitments or close family ties, visiting historic places and popular holiday resorts was what he enjoyed the most.

Over his years of travel to many poor nations, he was often cheated by those who were mainly out to swindle tourists. However, in spite of this, he still maintained a compelling desire to revisit some of these countries.

When meeting other tourists who came to visit these poor nations for the first time, he often shared his past experiences, telling them to be watchful of those who wanted to take advantage of them. He emphasized one particular incident when a taxi driver charged eight dollars to take him to a historic site, and then promised to return later to pick him up. But the driver never showed up, forcing him to take another taxi back to his hotel. On this return trip, he was again tricked by the driver who took the longest route back to make him pay a higher fee.

In some countries, he discovered that even seeking directions from some of the inhabitants was problematic, for some were reluctant to tell him where to go, but when he offered them money as an inducement, they were willing to take him to the exact place he wanted to visit.

Listening to the complaints of some poor people who blamed the ruling government for not doing enough to help them, he was not totally convinced by what they said, for he discovered that many were simply lazy and not keen to educate or uplift themselves.

Seeing the level of poverty in some of these nations, Romel did not harbor any ill feelings for their people, for he honestly believed that while some swindled tourists, the majority was willing to do any type of menial work to earn a living.

Many foreigners who were robbed on a visit to some of these poor nations said to Romel that they would never come back to visit such a place. This greatly saddened Romel, for he knew that the money gained from tourism contributed a great deal to the development of some of these poor nations.

Romel believed that there was something he could do to help the poor in a country that he loved, so he decided to invest all the money he had into the building of a fabulous holiday resort where foreigners could come and enjoy themselves. This would take three years and at the end, he would create a marvelous place for tourists to visit.

During the creation of this resort, hundreds of people were employed and Romel ensured that they were all paid well. Everyone who worked for him was pleased with the way he treated them, since they were made to feel important in the planning and building of the resort.

When the resort was finally completed, Romel hired a new set of local people to perform various duties to make it a heaven for tourists. To ensure the safety of foreigners, he set up his own taxi service to transport them to wherever they wanted at a fair price. Soon this resort became very popular, and Romel began to make huge profits from it.

Over the years, he became very wealthy, and his demeanor

slowly began to change, as he associated more closely with influential people who came to visit the resort. By mingling more often with the upper class, he gradually began to distance himself from the ordinary people who worked for him. A somewhat snobbish Romel found less time to communicate with his employees who contributed so much to his success. Having so much wealth, he became quite conceited and grew unfriendly with those he considered inferior.

Eventually many disenchanted employees began to gossip that the only time Romel met them was when their services were no longer required. And he only did this to give them some justification for their dismissal and to make it look as though he were going to miss them. Many who were unhappy with the way they were treated after Romel became well established made critical remarks, claiming that it was their efforts that made him so wealthy.

Over the years, Romel became the type of employer who was not too friendly with his employees, believing they would be less productive if they considered him of the same status as themselves. In short, he simply wanted everyone to know that he was the boss and they should respect him. It seemed that the more wealth he acquired, the more tightfisted he became, for he no longer gave pay increases to his employees. Because of this parsimony, many grew to dislike Romel and in private conversations continued to ridicule him. Sadly, however, one morning his employees were all surprised to hear that Romel had suddenly become very ill and was admitted to a hospital. Those employees who disliked him had harsh words, claiming that with his sudden illness he was paying for his sins. However, days later when they came to know that he was diagnosed with cancer and had only a couple of months to live, they all became deeply concerned. They feared that if Romel died, they would all be out of a job.

In the following weeks, no one said anything negative about Romel and all wished that he would recover from his illness. In the meantime Romel grew greatly distressed by the news that he was going to die. In hospital, he began to reflect on life, thinking that even with all his wealth nothing could save his life. He could not comprehend how such an unfortunate thing could happen to him at a point in life when everything had been going so well.

One day while lying in bed in a sorrowful mood, he met an elderly man who came to clean his room. The man instantly recognized Romel as his former boss, and happily introduced himself as Toby. When Romel looked carefully at Toby, he recognized him as one of his employees who used to perform most of the menial work on the resort.

Toby was a simple man and getting the opportunity to talk to his former boss was something he had always wished for. He wanted very much to tell Romel the reason why he suddenly walked off the job at the holiday resort many years ago. He explained that because he did menial work, some employees who were in senior positions treated him unfairly when asking him to clean the washrooms, sweep the floors and dispose of their garbage. Toby claimed that if he had gone to Romel to complain about being treated with contempt, Romel would favor others over him because he was the least educated.

Romel listened attentively to what Toby had to say and realized that he had distanced himself too much from his employees to the point where he cared little about their feelings. Though Toby had worked for him for such a long time, Romel had never uttered polite words such as hello or good morning to him. Saddened by this, Romel regretted not getting to know Toby who had served him faithfully over the years. He came to realize that sickness and death have no barriers, for even if one is wealthy and proud, all will experience these sorrows.

Knowing that his former boss was going to die, Toby felt sorry for him and told Romel not to worry about the past because Romel had never mistreated him. What troubled him the most were those employees who treated him as if he were stupid, and it was unfortunate that he had to complain about them at a time when his former boss was gravely ill.

During Romel's stay in hospital many of his close associates made numerous phone calls to talk about his illness, but none of them came to visit him. This bothered Romel a great deal as he really wanted to see his old business associates to talk about matters or events worth remembering. Disappointed, Romel wished that his friends would stop calling to find out how he was feeling. He commented to Toby that it would be useless for them to attend his funeral when he died, for when he was sick and lonely, none of them came to see him.

As Romel pondered each day about life, his views were mixed, thinking that though his life might be considered a short one, he had made the most of it. He was pleased that over the years he had enjoyed life to its fullest, for apart from being wealthy and educated, he did practically everything he desired to make life a happy experience. However, there was one thing that he deeply regretted, and that was being unable to control his ego and snobbish attitude which developed as a result of his insatiable appetite for wealth in the later stage of his life.

In these months, Romel's health seriously deteriorated and each day Toby came into his room to comfort him by offering words of hope. Romel developed a great deal of respect for Toby, the only one who cared about him, and he admired his sincerity. Sadly, Romel grew weaker each day and passed away early one morning. Though there was no blood relationship between them, for Toby it was as if someone closely related to him had died.

During the period of mourning, Romel's distant relatives and close business associates came to pay their respects at the funeral. Toby felt disappointed because everyone now appeared to really care for Romel. They all spoke well of his achievements and emphasized how much they would miss him.

Several weeks later, something unbelievable happened that changed Toby's life. A legal representative contacted him to say that before Romel died, he had made a will and left his entire estate to Toby.

Toby was very excited when he got the astonishing news and immediately began thinking about what to do with all the money he had inherited. Being uneducated and having no knowledge of managing a business, he did not want to take any chances investing his money. So he ignored everyone who advised him about investments and simply deposited all the funds into a bank account.

A few weeks later, Toby made a surprise decision to close down the entire holiday resort he inherited from Romel and put everything up for sale. Over a hundred people immediately lost their jobs, which made everyone furious. However, Toby was not interested in what anyone had to say about him, for this was his way of getting back at those who had mistreated him in the past.

When Toby's relatives heard that he had inherited a huge amount of money, they all began asking him for a portion of it. Believing that Toby was not capable of making financial decisions, they all wanted to advise him how to spend and invest his money. As Toby pondered about what to do with his riches, some of his relatives who were impatient claimed that they would never speak to him again unless he shared his wealth. Toby's life became so stressful that he began to suffer a great deal of mental torment. His blood pressure increased dramatically, and he collapsed one day and died, leaving all his wealth behind and many wondering who would inherit it all.

A Sage's Dream

A deeply religious man walked several miles each day on the plains towards Sodom in search of followers who would adhere to religious tenets which he believed were revelations from God. While on a journey to a remote village on a hot, humid day, he sat down under a shady tree to contemplate ways of getting unbelievers to accept God, whom he believed had created human beings. During this quiet contemplation, he fell asleep and had a dream that was edifying and unforgettable. He dreamt that God had given him a huge piece of land in paradise because of his good deeds on Earth. It was a place of immense beauty, filled with flowers, rivers of wine, and a single tree that was laden with luscious fruits.

While admiring the heavenly surroundings, he was suddenly taken aback by a mysterious voice, claiming to be that of Satan. Seeing no one and thinking that he was being tempted by the devil, he angrily shouted, "Get away!" The devil instantly replied, "Do not get angry for I am only here to reason with you. Listen to what I say and you will be wiser than those you adore."

The sage cried out loud, "O Lord my creator, protect me from Satan!" The devil politely said, "Don't be misled, for human beings were not created by God, instead it is humankind who created God by imagining Him to be either a divine spirit, something infinite or a man who sits on a throne."

The mysterious voice of the devil went on to say that while humankind created God with their minds to signify all that is righteous, they also created him to signify all that is wicked. He explained that in this dualistic view, human beings have a choice to follow either him or God.

To convince the sage, Satan claimed that in primeval times, human beings associated God with various aspects of nature and perceived God to be the divine mother of all. And to remind them of Her, they made statues depicting Her as a female with huge breasts and hips as a symbol of fertility. Today, however, with men being the stronger and more forceful sex, for the majority of worshippers God is perceived to be a powerful male who judges all mortal beings. Satan added that in ancient times it was believed that both the good and the wicked would go to hell or the underworld after death. This did not seem right to humans, hence the idea of rewards for doing good was introduced. A heaven for those who perform good deeds was believed to be above, while hell for the wicked was considered below.

Hearing only the voice of Satan in this celestial abode and not being able to see him in a physical form, the sage was absolutely bewildered. As he pondered over what the devil said, there was a brief period of silence. Then Satan claimed that because everyone is likely to commit sin, he had more followers than God. The sage became outraged and began to kick wildly, as though he were striking the devil. To this Satan commented, "What you are doing is evil and I am glad to have you as one of my followers. You are no different from many of the ancient prophets you adore, for they and their followers have conquered, killed and robbed others of their possessions." The sage, greatly angered by what he heard, rudely said, "Leave this place and go away for the Lord wants me to dwell here!" Satan replied, "I was born here, and it is not fair for me to leave my homeland, simply because God had promised you this land."

The sage was very uneasy about dwelling with the devil on the same land and became totally confused, thinking that this might not be paradise but a place on Earth. Looking around, he saw rivers of wine and felt thirsty. As he lowered his head to drink, the devil stopped him saying, "Do not drink for you will get drunk and lose your senses. Instead of wine, pick a fruit from the tree and eat it, for in doing so you will become knowledgeable. I do not hate you, but respect you for being the one who created me."

The story of Adam and Eve suddenly dawned on the sage, and he refused the fruit. The devil then softly said, "No one can harm you for eating this fruit, for it is fresh and pure. It is what you harbor in your mind that is making this fruit tainted. Eat it and you will feel invigorated. It will give you energy to think clearly, and from this you'll know the difference between right and wrong."

Soon, the sage became very hungry and looking around once more, he saw no other form of food but the fruits from the single tree that the devil spoke of. Not given much of a choice, he finally made up his mind and picked a fruit from the tree. Having eaten it, he suddenly felt refreshed and began to think of ways to get the devil off the land which he believed God had promised him.

Becoming furious once more at having to dwell with the devil on the same land, he began to kick wildly as though he were striking Satan. The devil affectionately said, "You are filled with anger and this will soon turn to hate, and from hatred you will try to kill me. And like those who advocate violence and kill in the name of God, you too will become my follower. I am a figment of your imagination, hence it is easy to blame me for your sins. If you kill me you will lose your job as a preacher because there will be no more evil and no one to blame."

In trying to reason with the sage, Satan claimed that he was pleased with the occupation humans had given him, to reason with God and to test the loyalty of His followers. He denied that he would punish anyone for their wrongdoings; instead, God and His angels carry out all forms of torture. This made the sage furious and he instantly denied it. The devil then said, "The Lord has commanded some prophets to destroy cities, kill or force the inhabitants out, yet the same God declares, 'Thou shall not kill. Some rules you claim God wants you to abide by are too rigid for human beings to follow. Think of how difficult it would be if God had to abide by His own rules."

The sage, realizing that the devil had no physical form, began to ponder on other means of getting rid of Satan. He decided to plead with the devil by politely asking him to leave this heavenly abode so that he could dwell in peace. Satan said, "I will only leave if you give up your belief in my existence and accept the fact that you are responsible for your own evil actions."

The sage carefully thought about it and said, "Though there are elements of truth in what you say, I cannot go against my religious teachings which claim the existence of the devil, for I will be punished for disbelieving. I am not afraid of you, Satan, for the Lord will always help and protect me. I have faith in God my creator, whom I believe can perform miracles such as curing sick people."

The devil answered, "What you say defies reason, for casting demons or me, Satan, out of people cannot cure them of disease. Don't be fooled, for there is no God who can help you, for all the ancient prophets you adore have suffered death on Earth. If they cannot save themselves, how can they save you? Do not rely on prayer to save you but seek peace within yourself and with others and you will find it comforting. There is no proof that the scriptures you abide by are the words of God, for they were either spoken or written by wise and intelligent men. Let the existence of God be based on the evidence of reason and nature, and you will become tolerant of all. You are indeed loyal to the God you've created; however, think of how much more knowledge you would gain if you allow me to remain in the same abode with you. God is not human-like as you perceive Him to be, and by reasoning with yourself, you will come to know that you've created God and Satan. When you accept God as the universe itself, there will be no prejudice regarding the color or gender of God."

The sage, holding firm to his beliefs, then said to Satan, "You are the chief enemy of God and it would be wrong for me to keep you as a friend." The devil replied, "When humans created me at first, I was a close associate of God, but later humans accused me of being bad and threw me into combat with God. Today, however, I am grateful to humankind, for they speak less of me being in conflict with God. Instead I feel sorry for God, since He now has to struggle with the sins of humanity which seem unending. Accept me as a friend and I will always be there to test your judgment of what is fair or unjust. Do not think of me as an evil spirit, for the true devils are humans who perform ungodly acts." In closing, Satan affectionately said, "When you awake from this dream you may choose either to acknowledge my existence or relinquish it."

The sage suddenly awoke and started to reflect on his dream. His inner conscience drove him to think that Satan might be right in many ways, but as a religious man, he could not accept what the devil said. He felt that even though some people use religion at their own convenience and do not read the scriptures, it is important for them to say they believe in God so that others will consider them normal and less sinful than nonbelievers. As hypocritical as this may sound, it seemed better for him not to accept the rational thinking of the devil, for if what he believed in was proven false, he would become greatly depressed.

Turbulent Minds

Stanley James was a shrewd professor who had spent over fourteen years teaching students on human behavior. From his studies, he concluded that each individual's desire and level of mental discipline are what determines the way they behave under different circumstances. Stanley's objective in this later stage of his life was to evaluate the behavior of his students in an effort to find the one who was most disciplined in speech and conduct. This, he believed, would help him to determine what the right standards are for others to emulate.

The class Stanley taught was comprised of students from various walks of life, and in order to test their level of mental discipline, he decided to get them to express their views on the subjects of religion and politics. In conversations with his students, Stanley purposely disagreed with some of their views to see how they would react. Judging from their reaction on these sensitive issues, he discovered that most of them were adamant about their beliefs.

Stanley observed that those who held steadfast to their religious beliefs seemed to be the most unyielding, for they often became argumentative and very disturbed when he tried to tell them that what they believed in did not make rational sense. Others who were intelligent and had moderate beliefs were less argumentative, as they often nodded their heads to show that they agreed with most of what he had to say. Though Stanley tried to provoke them by saying things which did not make sense, they remained very reserved in speech. He thought they were not sincere, but simply wanted to make a good impression by pretending to respect his views.

Amid various discussions with his students, he discovered that only two of them showed a great deal of mental discipline when they tried to reason with him. However, when he pretended not to yield to their reasoning, they eventually became frustrated at not being able to convince him.

Unable to find anyone with the ideal mental discipline to have the right conduct in nearly all circumstances, he decided to change his method, by putting himself to the test to see how he would be affected when rejected or criticized. He did this by performing a series of pious acts to make people believe that he was someone worthy of respect.

Stanley, now trying to harbor only righteous thoughts, renounced his profession, and with the money he had saved over the years, he created a charitable organization with the help of a few people who were kind at heart. However, because of his new occupation and this sudden change in his behavior, he was severely criticized by those who knew him, for they assumed that he was acting for personal gain. In spite of all the condemnation, Stanley managed to control his temper and not become agitated by what others said. Only a few people praised him for trying to do something good for humanity, and they were the ones who became his friends.

Soon Stanley developed a strong following of people with good intentions and a commitment to help the needy. When criticized at times, he felt a little annoyed since he honestly believed that his critics never took the time to look into what he and others were doing to help the impoverished. Through it all he maintained a great deal of mental discipline, and he became a quiet and humble person.

As the head of this charitable organization, Stanley became

very popular, and most of the praise about the good work of the organization was directed at him. However, such compliments meant little, as he was a humble person not interested in any rewards for his good deeds.

Over the years, Stanley continued to work assiduously for the betterment of those in need, and soon won the hearts of every member of the organization, who honestly felt that he was a man worthy of respect. However, amid the good work, a shocking thing happened that rocked the entire organization, causing it to be condemned by the community. One of the senior and most trusted members, Trevor Morrison, was accused of fraud. It was discovered that for years, he had been stealing money from the organization that was entrusted to him.

Trevor was severely criticized by every member of the organization except for Stanley, who was greatly distressed by what had happened. Trevor was a trusted friend and the news came as a complete surprise. Stanley compassionately felt it would be wrong for him to condemn his friend whom he had worked closely with over the years. Since he would not denounce Trevor, other members of the organization began to call for his resignation, claiming that what Stanley supported was wrong and that he seemed to have no intention of stopping it.

Deeply concerned about being criticized and feeling terribly ashamed of what others said, he relinquished his duties at the organization and went to a cloister to contemplate. Stanley began to re-think what had suddenly gone wrong within the organization. He slowly realized that by not opposing what was wrong, he was collaborating with evil. With this in mind, he denounced Trevor and demanded that he be tried in a court of law for the wrong he had done.

From the moment Stanley condemned Trevor, other

members of the organization he once headed began to thank him. They were happy to hear that he wanted Trevor brought to justice for the embezzlement. They encouraged Stanley to rejoin the organization, and wanting to see it remain successful, he willingly accepted their offer.

As everyone now joined in condemning Trevor, Stanley observed how his temperament and that of his associates began to change. Wanting to see justice served, he developed a strong dislike for Trevor. And as he reflected on this, he came to realize how his mental discipline was diminishing amid his desire to see Trevor put in prison.

With a date now set for Trevor's court trial, everyone wanted to hear what punishment would be imposed. However, as they waited patiently, Stanley and his associates received astonishing news that Trevor had suffered a severe heart attack and died. It was believed that after Trevor had been accused of fraud, he became greatly stressed from fear of being incarcerated.

Everyone within the organization stopped criticizing Trevor to show respect for the deceased. During this period of mourning, Stanley and his associates visited Trevor's home to offer their condolences to his family. Their behavior was totally hypocritical, for while paying their respects, they began scrutinizing the fabulous home and the luxurious cars that Trevor owned. They assumed that Trevor had acquired it all from the money he had stolen from the organization. One might have thought that they would wait until the funeral was over to discuss what they saw. But they immediately began to gossip about seeking legal means of getting back a sizeable portion of Trevor's estate.

After the funeral, Stanley worried about how complicated matters were becoming, believing that there would be a legal battle in claiming Trevor's assets. While he was deliberating about this, it suddenly dawned on him that it might not be possible to acquire the mental discipline he set out to achieve, for with each of the problems he encountered, he not only experienced a degree of mental fatigue, but his mood also varied.

Stanley felt that for him not to uphold what is just meant that he did not believe in fairness. To him justice should be served on the basis of reasoning as opposed to harsh criticism. Analyzing it all, Stanley came to believe that no mortal being could acquire all the qualities of what may be termed the ideal person, for at some point in life, everyone is likely to be criticized or encounter problems that will distress or annoy them.

Tyranny and Freedom

From a busy market place in an underdeveloped nation, a distressed fisherman named Frank Zoba saw each day scores of people applying for a visa to go to America. Having been turned down twice by immigration for not meeting the requirements to go to the United States, Zoba prayed each day for something propitious to happen, as he had grown weary of living under a totalitarian government.

It was when Marco Hernandez was elected that things drastically changed in his homeland. Under his dictatorship rule, hundreds of thousands of people wanted to leave this poor nation, fearing a tyrant who was quick to punish anyone who spoke ill of his government. For Zoba, deprived of his fundamental rights and not able to speak freely, life was very stressful. In the past, he had twice been arrested and punished for collaborating with a group of people in condemning Hernandez, and since then, he had remained quiet amid all the dishonesty. In moments of despair, Zoba often reflected on one mistake which he regretted, for as a teenager, he supported the socialist ideologies of Hernandez while having his mind set on going to America to live.

With no hope of coming to America the legitimate way, Zoba decided to seek illegal means. A close friend introduced him to the leader of a smuggling ring who claimed that for ten thousand dollars, he could secretly get Zoba and his family into America. However, after hearing the phenomenal cost for him and his family, he decided that only he would go on this challenging journey. With his mind set on going to America without his wife's knowledge, Zoba secretly withdrew all the money he had in the bank to pay the traveling costs.

Finally, the day came for him to leave his homeland. The arrangements were to take a flight to Cuba and from there, board another aircraft to Canada and then on to America.

On the first part of his journey to Cuba, he carried only a small bag of clothing and a few photographs of his wife and children. Aboard the aircraft, Zoba kept thinking about his family whom he had left behind, but he was optimistic, believing that if he got through to live in America, he would then sponsor the rest of his family.

Arriving in Cuba, he was picked up at the airport by a stranger who recognized him by the color of his shirt as arranged. Zoba was then taken to a private house where he was given some food and then told that at nightfall, he would be given a raft to set sail to America. Zoba became outraged and began yelling at the stranger, claiming that he could not go by sea for he was promised to be put onto another aircraft. The stranger claimed that he did not know anything about such arrangements, for he was simply told to provide Zoba with a raft and see him off. Zoba soon realized that he was tricked and now had no other choice but to make this journey by sea.

At nightfall, the stranger gave him a bottle of water and some food, then briefed him about the route. Soon Zoba was on a lonely journey at sea, and through it all, he kept thinking about his fellow countrymen who were suffering at home because of the horrific deeds of a tyrant and his supporters. He vowed that if he got to live in America, he would do everything within his power to ensure that Hernandez would be ousted from office.

Finally, after a long and turbulent journey at sea, his raft washed up onto the American shore and he felt greatly relieved.

However, before he could make up his mind about which direction to go, he saw a group of armed men running towards him. They were law enforcement agents who quickly surrounded him and took him to a secluded area where he was quarantined and questioned. These security officers, believing that he was on a sabotage mission and had accomplices, began to interrogate him. He was appalled by the way he was treated, punched and kicked several times by four guards who wanted him to admit that he was a saboteur. This frightening experience ended two days later when Zoba was approached by a man who was neatly dressed and claimed to be his legal representative. This lawyer documented his unfair treatment and then went public with the matter. When people heard how Zoba was mistreated and the sacrifice he made to come to America, they became sympathetic. With the strong support Zoba got from the American public, who severely criticized those who mistreated him, all the negative feelings he had about America changed. It was now clear to him that the four guards who abused him had taken the process of interrogation into their own hands, and it would be unfair to blame the entire nation for their actions.

Days later, news of Zoba's escape spread to his native land. Supporters of the corrupt government at home became furious when they heard of his escape to America, since they disliked that nation very much. His wife and children were in shock when they heard the news and honestly felt that he had abandoned them. However, Zoba later wrote them a letter telling them not to worry, for as soon as he got through to live in America, he would provide them with financial support.

Two weeks later, Zoba's legal representative told him that he could claim refugee status. With the lawyer's help, as well as the immigration authorities considering all the suffering he went through, Zoba was granted landed immigrant status a few months later. This was a dream come true for Zoba who was excited about living in America. Now that he was in a country in which there were more opportunities to better himself, Zoba found a job and began saving his money in preparation to sponsor his wife and children.

After several months, Zoba began to make contact with some of his fellow countrymen and became vocal in condemning the unfair practices in his native land. He soon got involved in numerous demonstrations, protesting and demanding that America remove the dictator from his native land. What he had to say did not attract much attention from the American government and this greatly angered him and his friends. These organized demonstrations soon got ugly and on two occasions, Zoba and his supporters burned the American flag. This certainly angered the majority of Americans who watched it on the news. Now Zoba found himself in conflict with the law and was advised that if he continued with such violent demonstrations, he could be deported back to his homeland. Zoba became very concerned and stopped protesting, fearing that if he were ever deported, he would surely be imprisoned and tortured in his native land.

In the following months, Zoba became a changed man and abided the law. He continued to work assiduously, and with time his wife and children through sponsorship were able to join him in America. This made his wife very happy, as she was now free to promote her culture and to practice her beliefs. They became a prosperous family with a beautiful apartment and a fair amount of savings.

Over the years, his children, two daughters and a son, grew up to be young adults who were fairly well educated. His eldest daughter later met and fell in love with an American soldier, and after months of getting to know each other, they got married, making Zoba very pleased. Unfortunately, three days after they were married, Zoba's son-in-law Nathan was called to serve his country in a war with a nation that was ruled by a brutal dictator. Zoba became very concerned, afraid that if Nathan were killed in this war his daughter would become a widow. Trying to encourage Nathan to refrain from his duty, Zoba told him that there was not enough justification for America to go to war, even though he knew that this dictator was much more brutal and dangerous than Hernandez.

After listening attentively, Nathan explained that his reason for going to war was to protect the rights and freedoms that Zoba enjoyed in America. Nathan went on to say that because of the suffering this dictator had inflicted on his own people, as well as his advocating the killing of American citizens, he viewed this as a justification for war. Zoba felt uncomfortable, for this made him feel as if he were not loyal to the country where he now lived. Realizing that it could be a sensitive issue, he refrained from further argument with his son-in-law. Seeing that there was nothing he could do to get Nathan to change his mind, he let the decision be made by the young soldier. Even though he did not support America's involvement in this war, he wished his son-in-law well on his combat mission.

Over the coming months, Nathan kept in contact with his wife through letters, and in each of them, he mentioned that he would be coming home soon, believing that this war would only last a few months. However, his wife received distressing news one day that Nathan was killed in the line of duty. This news greatly saddened Zoba and his family. He was deeply touched by the loss, and amid his grief, the words of Nathan that he was going to war to protect the rights and freedoms that Zoba enjoyed in America, kept ringing in his ears.

In the following months, Zoba continued to lament over the death of Nathan, and it was not until he received news from his native land that his father was dying that these sorrowful feelings for Nathan temporarily halted. He now began to worry about his sickly father whom he hadn't seen for over ten years.

Since the old corrupt government was still in power, Zoba was reluctant to visit his homeland, fearing he might be persecuted. However, seeing that he had been over a decade in America, he felt that it was unlikely for the supporters of the corrupt regime to remember him. So he decided to visit his father.

Unfortunately, as soon as he arrived in his native land, supporters of Hernandez recognized him and immediately he was arrested. He feared that he would be punished and might never make it back to America. Without any trial, he was immediately thrown into prison for an indefinite period. He was occasionally beaten and reminded never to escape to America.

During these worrisome years, occasionally he reflected on the dialogue he once had with his son-in-law, and deliberated on matters relating to U.S. involvement in solving some of the problems of other nations. He developed mixed feelings, for on occasions when he was tortured in prison he blamed America for not going to war with Hernandez who ruled his native land. On other occasions, it seemed to him that the more America got involved with the problems of other nations, the more it would be criticized, and perhaps it was doing the right thing by ignoring Hernandez. Thinking about the millions of people worldwide who had fled their homeland to come to America, he felt sorry for those who could not escape persecution or hardships. Having lived in America, Zoba felt that the negative views of America by the media in his native land were misleading, for he found America to be a helpful nation, and that others envied its freedoms. Believing that he would one day be killed, he wished that some other nation besides America would come and liberate his fellow compatriots. But he had doubts about this, coming to think that those who suffered under dictators had no other choice but seek an opportunity to leave.

As Zoba continued to lament over his concerns, he was drawn to think about the impermanence of things, and he was hopeful that Hernandez would be toppled someday. However, amid this optimism a new concern developed and this seemed to worry him the most. Reflecting on past dictators who were brought to justice, Zoba found it difficult to understand why some people who were aware of the atrocities a tyrant had committed seemed willing to forgive him when he was put on trial for his evil doings. What drives some people to support a tyrant in spite of all his wrongdoings was something that Zoba would continue to ponder on for years to come.

Nammu's Abode

It was New Year's Day when the Reverend Simon Wakely attended church to give his farewell speech to a packed audience. In this homily, the eighty-four-year old Simon emphasized all the good he had done on Earth and made a wish that he be granted immortality after death. Those who attended the ceremony acknowledged most of what he had to say, since for decades he had done a remarkable amount of good for humanity.

As Simon stood on the podium glorifying the name of God amid applause from the congregation, he suddenly collapsed onto the floor, apparently having suffered a severe heart attack. As he lay motionless on the ground, many with implicit faith began praying for him not to die. However, while they prayed with sincere devotion, a few senior church officials immediately decided to get medical help.

Surprisingly, what happened to Simon this day did not last very long, for twenty minutes later he regained consciousness and asked those around him to help him to get on his feet. Minutes later, Simon had recuperated; he slowly walked up to the podium and announced that he had something important to say.

In this speech, Simon claimed that what had just happened to him seemed like he had died and then suddenly came back to life. During his speech, he suddenly felt very weak and his heartbeat seemed to stop. He instantly woke up in a heavenly abode where there were countless people. Among them were his wife and many of his friends who had died decades ago. Seeing his loved ones, his heart became filled with joy, but since he was very old they could not recognize him or recall ever meeting him before.

Simon commented that it puzzled him a great deal that everyone he met thought of him as someone new who came to join them in feasting in heaven. People eating fruits, drinking wine, milk and honey, and having fun with thousands of beautiful maidens who served them, all appeared similar to the heaven many on Earth talked about and wanted to go to after their demise.

Looking at countless people feasting in this celestial abode, he felt greatly disappointed, for it was no different from what humans do on Earth. He discovered that people who were young seemed to be the happiest, while those who were very old appeared bored and depressed, and too feeble to keep up with all the fun and feasting.

Simon soon fell into a melancholy mood believing that he had died, and from thinking about his loved ones who were still alive on Earth. He wished that he could come back to life and be reunited with his relatives and friends. Being unhappy in heaven, Simon decided to inquire from others about the place where God resided. He soon found out that God was not very far from him and was seated on a soft, high chair. From this place, the Lord quietly observed everyone who partook in the ongoing feast.

As Simon looked up to see the Lord, his heart became filled with love to discover that the Almighty was a tall, dark lady who was extremely beautiful. He immediately prostrated below Her and then humbly asked Her to disclose Her name. She politely replied, Nammu, and expressed how pleased She was with his conduct in heaven, for he seemed to have a great deal of control over his desires. Nammu went on to say that of all human beings, Simon impressed Her the most, since everyone else who came to heaven thus far had neglected Her. She complained that the human beings in heaven seem more interested in eating, drinking and having fun with the maidens, and the only time they came to visit her was to ask what more there was to enjoy in heaven after becoming bored with doing the same things repeatedly.

Grateful for the opportunity to meet the Lord, Simon began to plead with Nammu to send him back to Earth so that he could tell others about what he saw in this heavenly place. Without hesitating, Nammu told him that because he was loyal to Her, he deserved to be given whatever he wished. However, She cautioned Simon that what he saw was not the real heaven but a place She had created for human beings to enjoy after death, and She was allowing them to take pleasure, since it was the reward they craved the most for doing good on Earth. Nammu affectionately said to him that She was the mother of all, and that everything he had seen on Earth and now in heaven was Her revealing it all in infinite diversity. She told Simon that this form he saw Her in was one that pleases humans, and if he wished, She could show him the true heaven. Simon became excited and begged Her to reveal it. Nammu stepped down from Her chair and told Simon to look into Her eyes. As he did so, he was instantly mesmerized by what he saw. From her eyes, he could see the sun, numerous planets and boundless places of incredible beauty. Each time he stared into Her eyes there was something new and fascinating, leading him to believe that everything one can see or think of exists within the Almighty. Nammu then said to him that because of his good deeds on Earth, She would give him the choice of becoming an integral part of God or returning to Earth to be with his loved ones.

Having seen the incredible power of Nammu, practically revealing every corner of the universe in Her eyes, Simon contemplated what to do. If he accepted what Nammu said about being an essential part of the Almighty, he would no longer get to see his loved ones on Earth. To Simon it would be a noble act if he shared his heavenly experiences with people on Earth so that they might have a better understanding of what God encompasses. With this in mind, he prostrated before Nammu and told Her that he would like to go back to Earth. Nammu granted him his wish, and it was at this point that Simon suddenly regained consciousness. Simon immediately made a pledge that after he died on Earth, he would accept Nammu's offer to become an integral part of the Almighty.

Back on Earth, after listening attentively to what Simon had to say, many began to dispute his claims that the Almighty was a beautiful female, since it had been instilled in their minds that God was male. What Simon said was considered blasphemy by the majority who told him that the devil had corrupted his mind. In anger many threw objects at him and demanded that he get out of the church immediately. Simon was totally shocked by the violent behavior of churchgoers. Amid the uproar, he suddenly suffered a severe heart attack and died.

What Simon said in church turned out to be a controversial subject among those who supported his claims and those who disapproved of them. While many debated the identity of God, others who were open-minded were drawn to think that God is that One which is totally devoid of gender.

My Children Bring Joy and Pain

Louise Johnson grew up in Queens, New York, where at age sixteen she bore a child out of wedlock. After Louise became pregnant, and after months of bitter quarrels over her pregnancy, her parents separated. Her father totally renounced her and her mother moved back to Guyana, claiming that Louise would have turned out better if she had been raised there.

Years after this turbulence with her parents had calmed down, Louise encountered a number of problems raising her son Malcolm, who over the years grew stubbornly perverse. When he was six, she received calls from Malcolm's teacher about his rude behavior at school, and about his habit of hitting other boys he disliked. For the young mother, it was tough having to work long hours and also to take care of a child who would not yield to parental authority.

Making her problems worse was that the child's father, who was only seventeen when they met, went into hiding on learning that Louise was pregnant. Louise strongly believed that his parents had secretly sent him to live with a relative in another county, taking for granted that they did not want him to get married and take the responsibility of raising a child.

In Queens, Louise shared a two-bedroom apartment with her grandmother who was Malcolm's babysitter and the one he was least hostile to. Here, Louise was very afraid of telling people about the problems she was having raising her child, fearing someone would report her to the police or social services. To win Malcolm's affection, she tried everything a loving parent could do to comfort her child. At times the extra attention pleased Malcolm, but this was ephemeral for when Malcolm got bored, he returned to the habit of pulling on the curtains and throwing his toys against the walls. When Malcolm did not get to do as he pleased, he tried to hurt his mother by pulling her hair. However, in spite of his impolite behavior, Louise tried her utmost to remain calm and not speak ill of her child.

Over the years, Louise regretted some of the mistakes she had made earlier in not completing her high school studies and in getting pregnant at an early age. Since there was little she could do to change this, she decided to work and save as much money as she could to provide Malcolm with a sound education when he grew up.

One summer it suddenly dawned on Louise to take Malcolm back to Guyana for a two-week holiday, hoping this would be fun for him and an opportunity to meet some of their relatives. As part of her preparation, she decided to take Malcolm shopping for summer clothing; however, even taking him out was problematic, for Malcolm ran wildly through the busy stores and even threw himself down on the floor, crying as though someone was hurting him. Confused by it all, Louise had to postpone her shopping and return home.

Finally, it was time for them to travel to Guyana and Louise was very excited to be going on a holiday. Arriving in Guyana, Malcolm was puzzled, for the surroundings were quite different from New York. The tropical plants, wooden buildings and the busy market places were all new to him. For the first couple of days, he kept close to his mother and was reluctant to go out in the yard to play with other boys. In this environment he felt insecure among strangers. His mother observed that there was absolutely no sign of aggressive behavior from Malcolm; though he was given lots of toys to play with, he never threw them about, rather he kept clinging to his mother's skirt most of the time.

A week later, Malcolm was getting less attention from relatives and now he appeared more open, as he began to mingle with other boys who usually came out in the evenings to play. For the first couple of days Malcolm was treated well by other children who wanted to make him feel happy during his short visit to Guyana. However, days later, he showed signs of aggression, returning to his old habit of hitting other boys, who could not comprehend this sudden change in his behavior. Because of this many young boys grew to dislike him and began to fight back. Now being taunted and treated in an unfriendly manner, Malcolm became afraid to go out of the house and play, so for the rest of his stay, he chose to stay indoors with his mother.

Finally, their two-weeks' stay in Guyana came to an end and, having said goodbye to their relatives, they departed for the United States. Returning home, Malcolm seemed more at ease, since he was happy to see his grandmother. On the first day, he was relatively quiet, very tired after the long journey. However, days later, he was back to his usual self of throwing his toys around and kicking the furniture in a rebellious manner. This kind of behavior was again worrisome for Louise, but she tried to stay composed since she honestly believed that Malcolm's behavior would change as he grew older.

Unfortunately, she did not get to witness these changes. One night, when for the first time she struck her child to punish him, the police were called in to investigate the matter. This happened one evening when Louise had returned from work and had asked her grandmother to purchase a few household items while she took care of Malcolm and prepared dinner. It was while granny was away that Malcolm again began throwing his toys about the house. After several warnings not to do so, Louise became angry and yelled at him. Then the most shocking thing happened as the six-year-old began pulling his mother's hair and scratching her on the face. This made Louise furious, and in anger she spanked him twice on his buttocks. Malcolm began to scream as if someone were trying to kill him. His high-pitched voice echoed through the corridor of the apartment building. One of Louise's neighbors, believing that someone was seriously harming the child, telephoned for the police.

Arriving at the scene, one of the officers ran over to calm down Malcolm who was weeping. Immediately, they began to question him about what had happened, and in reply Malcolm told the police that his mother had hit him. The police, concerned about the young boy's safety, further questioned if his mother had spanked him before. Sobbingly, he replied that Louise always hit him. Louise became very concerned since she realized that such an insincere answer from her son could get her into serious trouble with the law. She was now seriously questioned by police, and though she explained that it was the first time she had spanked her son, both officers did not believe her story.

Later that evening, Louise's grandmother returned from shopping and was appalled to see Louise crying and being questioned by police. Hearing what had happened, granny told the officers that what Malcolm had said about his mother was not true, but they did not believe her. The officers then decided to leave the child in the grandmother's custody until the next day, when arrangements would be made for a social worker to visit Louise to discuss what had happened.

On the following day, Louise was visited by a young social worker who began to question her about the dispute with her son. As they talked, Malcolm appeared in a happy mood as he sat on the floor playing with his toys. Soon it was Malcolm's turn to be questioned about how he was treated by his mother. This displeased Louise, as it appeared to her that the social worker was putting words into her son's mouth to hear all the negative things about her. What Malcolm had to say again came as a surprise, for he told the social worker that his mother always hit him. Louise was astonished by her son's remark, fearing that she could be investigated and charged for child abuse.

Towards the end of their meeting, the social worker somehow gave Louise the impression that she was very understanding, and that Louise would be contacted for another interview. After she left a dejected Louise contemplated what she had done wrong that caused her son to be so contumacious. It was quite distressing, since she realized that no one would believe her story after hearing what Malcolm had said.

Two weeks later, Louise was taken by complete surprise when law enforcement agents came knocking on her door to inform her that they were taking her son to a foster home. It was distressing for Louise and her grandmother, to have the young boy they cared for suddenly snatched away. Normally, the children's aid society would have done a thorough investigation of this matter. However, it appeared that they had taken into consideration how consistent the child was in claiming that his mother had always hit him.

To Louise, the dream of wanting to see Malcolm grow up to be educated suddenly came to a halt. She felt that she had been treated unfairly, that she was not the kind of parent who would seriously abuse their child out of anger.

Amid her grief, Louise resented the social worker who appeared so understanding, and yet recommended that her only child be taken away. Though she understood that this social worker was trained for the job, it did not seem right to her for an unmarried person to give counsel to others when they had never raised a child who was intransigent. She honestly felt that a levelheaded elderly person would have been better suited to deal with marital problems or cases of child abuse.

Over the following weeks, Louise became more distraught and was absent from work frequently. As a result, she lost her job which compounded her problems. What proved even more worrisome was a telephone call late one night from a relative in Guyana, telling her that her mother had suffered a heart attack and died. A distraught Louise immediately decided to travel to Guyana to attend her mother's funeral. Louise was met by relatives who seemed more interested in talking about what had happened to her son Malcolm than her mother who had died. They were very upset with the news that Louise was charged with abuse and had her child taken away when trying to discipline him.

A few days after the funeral, Louise's uncle, hearing about all that had gone wrong in Louise's life, offered her a job in a posh nightclub that he owned. Since things were not going well for Louise in America, she willingly accepted the offer. She then telephoned her grandmother in New York to tell her that she had found a job, and would be spending three months in Guyana before returning to the United States.

Louise proved to be hard-working and after two months, she was offered a senior position to manage the nightclub. She was very pleased with this job because she was paid and treated well by her uncle.

With life appearing less hectic, Louise decided not to return to the United States as she had planned. Being so taken up with her occupation, several months went by before Louise came to realize that she had over-stayed her time in Guyana, and for her to return to the United States meant she had to re-apply for landed immigrant status.

Working long hours at this nightclub in Guyana greatly eased Louise's worries. Being so busy at work kept her from worrying too much about her son. But before long, that motherly feeling of wanting to be with her child began to dwell on her mind once more, so she decided to re-apply to go back to the United States to live. After several months of waiting for her application to be processed, Louise received a letter from the immigration department indicating that she did not meet certain requirements which would allow her entry into the United States. It seemed that her long absence out of the country put her at a disadvantage. Once more, Louise fell into a state of despair and it would take months for her to realize that she must carry on in life, and remain hopeful that some day she would be reunited with her son.

Over the years, Louise saved a great deal of money, and she purchased a beautiful home in the city of Georgetown. During these years her grandmother in the United States had become quite sickly, and after months of being in and out of hospital, she sadly passed away one night in her sleep.

* * *

A decade later, Louise had grown much older; however, she was in good health and looked quite well for someone in her mid-thirties. In her spare time she read a great deal on the subject of human behavior, since she still wanted to know the reason for her son's rebellious behavior as a child.

One day while watching a talk show program, she saw a man named Charles Munroe giving a talk on human behavior and was very impressed with what he had to say. This weekly show made Munroe very famous, as he was an eloquent speaker who talked a great deal about ways to improve people's lives as well as topics of a philosophical nature. After months of watching him on television, she observed that the audience who listened to Munroe was mostly educated people in America, but here in Guyana, the ordinary citizens saw him as a man making millions of dollars, talking about poverty and the need to help others. To some people, Charles Munroe had found a way to get rich by simply acting the role of a nice guy.

The more Louise reflected on his show, the more Munroe came across as superficial. In her view, he was earning millions of dollars trying to make people feel a little guilt for not doing enough to help others, and at the same time, filling their heads with abstract ideas about searching for an inner peace to comfort them. She harbored one question: if such a wealthy celebrity were given her problems, how would he cope with them? After a while, Louise lost interest in the show and her thoughts shifted to finding some means of returning to America where she could be reunited with her son.

One night while working, Louise was astonished to see the celebrity Charles Munroe at the nightclub where she worked. With Munroe's head cleanly shaven and his beard neatly groomed, he looked quite mature. After talking with one of the waitresses who was tending to Munroe and his friends, she learned that they all came to Guyana on a holiday. Though Louise was no longer a big fan of Munroe, she did not want to lose the opportunity to meet the celebrity. As the manager of the nightclub, she hurried to his table to greet them.

At the club, Munroe and his associates were treated well and for their remaining stay in Guyana this became their favorite place to visit each night. He grew to like Louise more and more, and within days, a love relationship developed. Whatever qualities Louise did not like about Munroe when she watched his television program quickly faded away, as love seemed to cast away all her negative feelings about him.

By this time, Munroe's vacation in Guyana was coming to an end, but just before his departure, he proposed marriage to Louise. Though Munroe was much older than her, she was a woman in love and age made no difference. Despite this short courting, Munroe promised Louise that within a year he would return to Guyana to marry her.

Louise was much happier now, since it was also an opportunity for her to get back into the United States. Six weeks later, Louise discovered that she was pregnant, and she telephoned Munroe to let him know. Munroe was very pleased with the news. He told her that he could not come to Guyana immediately because he had signed a television contract which would last for eight months. Louise understood his commitment, and over the coming months they spoke frequently over the phone.

In June, Louise gave birth to a baby boy and she was happy, even though the delivery of this child would have been a little disappointing for some. Both of the infant's legs were deformed, which meant he would require a great deal of parental care. Louise was not overly concerned, for in spite of the child's physical condition, she was pleased with his birth. In her conversation with Munroe about the birth of their son, she never mentioned the child's physical deformity.

Eight months later when Munroe was expected to return to Guyana, Louise got a telephone call from him saying that he had signed another television contract, and was going to earn millions of dollars. Munroe promised that he would not let her down for as soon as his new two-year contract ended, he would come to Guyana. Once more, Louise was struck with disappointing news and was now left to take care of her disabled child alone. In spite of this, Louise remained hopeful for she strongly believed that Munroe would keep his promise.

Fortunately for Louise, raising this young boy was much easier than her previous child, since he had a pleasant personality and never showed any signs of unruly behavior. Though she had to work and take care of this child with the help of a babysitter, she enjoyed it very much as the young boy was always happy to see her after work.

Finally, Munroe's contract ended, and Louise received a phone call from him saying that he would be coming to Guyana to marry her, and to eventually take her and their son back to the United States where he had bought a fabulous home for them. Louise was delighted and a week later Munroe came to Guyana.

Arriving at Louise's home, Munroe was happy to see her and immediately he asked her to show him their son. When Munroe saw the young boy, he was instantly taken aback by the boy's physical deformity.

The disappointed look on Munroe's face was a concern to Louise, since she had to ask him repeatedly to pick the child up and hug him. Munroe did as he was told, not in a loving manner but a pretentious one. Louise became suspicious and asked him what was wrong. In reply, Munroe questioned Louise as to why she had kept the child's physical deformity a secret. Louise then recounted her earlier problems with an insubordinate child she bore out of wedlock, and how he was taken away from her after she had been accused of abusing him. She also explained that the birth of this disabled child brought her a great deal of happiness. And in her view, her child was just as good as anyone else's and his disability was insignificant. Considering all the problems she had with her first child, her disabled son was a blessing, for in him she saw all the qualities of a loving and contented child.

After listening to all this, Munroe looked even more bewildered, for he shook his head as if to say, he had gotten himself into a difficult situation where taking care of a disabled child was part of his responsibility. He was very disturbed by the fact that Louise had never mentioned to him that she had borne a child out of wedlock or about their disabled son. A somewhat confused Munroe told Louise that he needed some time to be by himself, since most of what he heard came as a complete surprise. He decided to go to a hotel which he had booked for the night and would return the next day to visit her.

Judging from the disappointed look on Munroe's face, Louise could not say what he was harboring in his mind. At his hotel, he secretly began making flight arrangements to leave Guyana as soon as possible. Being a wealthy celebrity who did not want to be burdened with this additional responsibility, his plan was to abandon both mother and child and return to the United States. Louise in the meantime began calling her relatives to tell them that she and Munroe were going to get married soon.

On Munroe's undisclosed journey to the airport, he kept urging the taxi driver to speed along the road, as he did not want to miss his flight. Sadly, the car he was traveling in collided with another and he was instantly killed. Soon it was news, and on practically every television channel, the death of Charles Munroe was made public. When Louise heard the shocking news she was devastated, and to also learn that he was leaving for the United States without telling her was heart-breaking.

Since he was a celebrity, there was rumor about Charles

Munroe and the affair he had with Louise Johnson in Guyana. It was a distressing period for Louise, as her neighbors began to gossip about her. Unable to cope with rumor, Louise sold her home and moved to the outskirts of Georgetown, where she began to live a quiet life.

Several weeks later, something propitious happened amid the series of misfortune Louise had encountered. One evening she heard a knock on her door. Opening it, she saw a tall, handsome man who introduced himself as Malcolm Johnson, wishing to meet his mother Louise Johnson. Louise became ecstatic and affectionately embraced him. He explained that it was through the news about Munroe's relationship with Louise, and the gossip about her early life, that he found out that Louise was his mother and where she lived. Finally, the long string of misfortunes Louise encountered came to an end, as she and her sons found happiness dwelling together. What pleased Louise the most was that Malcolm turned out to be educated and well–mannered as she had always wished.

Disloyalty and Revenge

West Palm Beach, Florida is a central region where a number of influential businessmen own some of the most fabulous homes in a neighborhood reserved mainly for the upper class of society. It was in one of these luxurious homes that Leslie Thompson, a fifty-three-year old businessman, lived with his beautiful wife Doreen.

Dwelling in an environment where most adults were very much into fitness and fashion, Doreen in this later stage of her life became driven with the desire to look more attractive. Leslie could not understand this sudden change in his wife's behavior, for when she was young and beautiful she was very reserved. She was never concerned with fitness or fashionable clothing until she reached age forty. In trying to comprehend this change in her, he concluded that his wife was competing with other well-to-do women in craving attention from anyone who would compliment or tell them how beautiful they looked.

Leslie was a generous man who loved friends, and at his palatial home, he threw lavish parties. These social gatherings were great fun for Leslie's friends, since he was hospitable every time they came to his home. These friends were very important to Leslie, because they were influential businessmen who took part in many of his financial deals. However, due to this sudden change in Doreen's demeanor, he became concerned that his friends could lose respect for her when under the influence of alcohol. He therefore advised his wife not to be too friendly with his business associates.

Doreen, much more outgoing than before, ignored much of what her husband had to say. She dressed as she pleased and liked the attention she was getting from Leslie's friends. Soon, Leslie grew jealous of his wife flirting with other men, and fearing that his friends would lose respect for her, he stopped inviting them to his home.

After several months like this, Doreen became resentful and was less affectionate to her husband. It appeared to Leslie that she was bored, for she seemed to miss the attention from his friends. But this was not the case for one day, he was thrown into a state of shock when he got a telephone call from Doreen, saying that she would not be coming home, and would be staying with her mother for an indefinite period. This was a stunning surprise for Leslie, and as soon as their telephone conversation ended, he speeded over to her mother's home.

At the house, Leslie started a frantic knock on the door. This made his mother-in-law very nervous for she kept asking, "Who is it? Who is it?" As she fumbled with the lock an angry Leslie yelled, "It's me! Open the door!" Upon recognizing his voice, she nervously opened the door. Leslie marched into the house shouting, "Where is Doreen?" His mother-in-law, very confused, softly said, "She is not here!" Leslie left and slammed the door, leaving his in-law totally bewildered by what might have gone wrong.

Over the next three days, Leslie frequently visited his mother-in-law's home looking for Doreen, but unfortunately, she never came to visit her mother. However, on the fourth day while Leslie was relaxing at home, he received a telephone call from his loyal friend Renaldo, telling him that his wife was having an affair with his boss, nicknamed Doug. Renaldo was the head chef of a posh restaurant which Doug owned, and it was here that Leslie had first met his wife.

Doug and Leslie were close friends for many years and Doug attended numerous parties at Leslie's home. Since Doug was a popular and well-respected businessman, Leslie took the news with silence, thinking that his relationship with his wife was over, and he could not afford to make too much of an issue out of it, fearing gossip.

Now alone, a dejected Leslie sat in his home contemplating what he had done wrong to cause his wife to suddenly abandon him. He found no reason to blame himself, but he did not want to accuse Doreen wrongfully. To confirm what his friend Renaldo had said was true, he decided to keep in close contact with the chef to find out when his wife came to meet Doug at the restaurant. This turned out to be valid, for one evening Renaldo secretly allowed Leslie into the kitchen of the restaurant to see the owner and Doreen together, enjoying a special meal which Doug had prepared for her.

Leslie was very hurt by what he saw and immediately became vindictive. Amid his rancor, he began to think of ways to kill his wife, and also about the consequences of committing murder. He realized that he could face the death penalty if caught, and he pondered on what would be the maximum prison sentence in the event that he was proven guilty of killing his wife. Days later, it suddenly dawned upon him that pleading insanity was one way of escaping the death penalty. And with this in mind, he decided to become the patient of a psychiatrist.

Meeting with the doctor, Leslie recounted all the events leading up to the love affair between his wife and Doug. After several visits to the psychiatrist, in order to deceive the doctor, Leslie told him that he was thinking about committing suicide, and that he had gotten a message from God to kill someone. To further confuse the doctor, Leslie occasionally chewed on the tie he wore around his neck and mumbled things which did not make sense. After repeatedly doing this on each visit, the psychiatrist came to conclude that Leslie was mentally sick and slowly going insane.

During the course of these visits to the doctor, Leslie began to work secretly with his loyal friend Renaldo on a plan to kill his wife. Collectively, they decided that one day when Doug prepared a special meal for Doreen, Renaldo would secretly poison her food and this would lead to Doug being accused of killing Doreen. To encourage Renaldo, Leslie promised to give him one hundred thousand dollars to poison his wife.

The plan to get rid of Doreen was put into effect one week later when Doug told Renaldo that he had invited Doreen to the restaurant for dinner, and he would be preparing a special meal for her. On that day, Renaldo did not come out of the kitchen to greet Doreen as he usually did, but pretended to be busy and allowed Doug to be the one serving her food.

Doug wanted Doreen to sample small portions of food that he cooked, so he frequently moved in and out of the kitchen to serve her. It was during one of these short breaks when Doug had left the kitchen that Renaldo quickly poisoned the main meal which Doug had prepared for Doreen. At the end of this meal, Doreen was not feeling well and asked Doug to take her to her mother's home. Later that evening, Doreen got seriously ill and before her mother could get help, she passed away.

The following day, the police began to conduct an investigation and at the end of it, Doug was arrested and charged with the death of Doreen. Based on the evidence that he was the one who had prepared the meal for Doreen, as well as the relationship they had, he was given a lengthy prison sentence. Leslie was very pleased with the outcome of this trial, finally getting the revenge he wanted.

When matters relating to Doug's trial had ended, Leslie

decided to make one final visit to his doctor to fake his insanity, and to pay him his medical fees. Accompanying him on this visit was his loyal friend Renaldo who waited patiently outside the doctor's office. During Leslie's conversation with the psychiatrist, the doctor politely asked him how long he knew the friend who was waiting outside. Leslie indicated that Renaldo was a close friend who worked for the man who had poisoned his wife, and after this visit both of them would be traveling to Ohio on business. The doctor offered his sympathy to Leslie.

While pretending to be insane, Leslie made one serious mistake by telling the psychiatrist that what had happened to his wife was the one evil act that God wanted someone to perform. This made the doctor suspect that the two of them had something to do with Doreen's death. He began to question Leslie about his companion Renaldo and where he was when Doreen was poisoned.

From what the doctor asked, it became clear to Leslie that he suspected them of murder and he might inform the police. Afraid of being caught, Leslie suddenly pounced on the doctor and began choking him. With a tight hold on his throat and a menacing look, Leslie squeezed with all his might until he no longer felt any struggle. He then slowly released his hands from the doctor's throat, and quickly checked his heartbeat to ensure that he was dead. Immediately, Leslie rushed out of the office to meet Renaldo whom he hurriedly told about the murder he had just committed.

Together, Leslie and Renaldo hurriedly drove to the airport to board an aircraft bound for Ohio. After they left, a patient who had come to visit the doctor discovered him dead and immediately contacted the police. With Leslie's medical files strewn on the table, he was clearly a suspect in this homicide.

An hour later, while they were waiting in the departure lounge of the airport, both of them were arrested.

After their trial, Renaldo was given a lengthy prison sentence and, based on the psychiatrist's records, Leslie was proven insane and sent to a mental asylum.

Now in a mental institution with mad people, Leslie continued to pretend to be insane, knowing that because of this, he would not face the death penalty. During this period, he spent most of his time quietly contemplating how to get out of this mental institution. After months of careful planning, Leslie began to behave normally, hoping that the officials would recommend that he be released from the institution based on his good conduct. Soon Leslie began to secretly instigate violence and hate among the patients so as to get them to quarrel and fight with one another. Whenever these disputes occurred, Leslie made it a habit to secretly call the guards to quiet them. At times when the situation got too much out of hand, Leslie himself settled disputes by acting in the role of a peacemaker.

In the coming years, Leslie turned this once-organized institution into a place of hell, as he continued to secretly instigate hate among insane people who could not comprehend what he was doing. As many officials came to like Leslie for being so helpful in settling disputes, he soon won their respect and was allowed to eat with the guards. Now that he was acting so responsibly, the majority of officials at the institution felt that he was no longer insane. Based on Leslie's good conduct, he finally got the freedom he wanted, for after five years in the asylum, he was declared medically sane and released.

Changes in Life

Louis Gárcia, a confirmed bachelor, was elected mayor after winning a closely fought election in the state of New Mexico. His narrow victory was largely due to the strong ethnic support he got from people of his own race. Having immigrated to a wealthy nation over fifteen years ago, his ambition was to play an important role in the development of his new homeland.

Dwelling in a multicultural society, Louis discovered that a high percentage of immigrants had a tendency to support politicians of their own kind, believing that they would be better represented. Louis, a considerate person, disliked this trend because he wanted to see every race treated fairly. Though he was happy to be voted mayor, he was not entirely pleased with the way he got elected, as many who supported him made race an issue during the election campaign.

After several months as mayor, Louis was frequently approached by some of his supporters seeking special favors pertaining to business, immigration and employment matters. Having a strong belief in fairness, Louis constantly tried to convince these people that he had limited powers and it would be wrong for him to show preference for people of his own race. Because of his adamancy to remain impartial, many who had voted for him began to criticize him sharply, claiming that as their mayor, he was doing absolutely nothing to help anyone. Then his political opponents joined in condemning him in an attempt to force him to step down from office. This kind of slander was something Louis greatly disliked about democracy. He believed that because the media have the freedom to ridicule the policy of an elected leader, those from foreign nations who watch the news might be led to think that this leader was dishonest. This kind of belittling, he believed, could make a democratically elected leader with good intentions sound more corrupt than some brutal dictators. Though Louis knew in his heart that he was honest, he feared that with so much political insult no one would trust him.

All the negative things people were saying made Louis greatly distressed, believing that such criticisms were seriously hurting his credibility. Unable to cope with rejection and the harsh condemnation, he decided after serving two years in office to relinquish his post as mayor and seek a new job.

After weeks of quiet deliberation over a good occupation to serve humanity, Louis decided to become a priest and live a life of celibacy. He believed that by having such an occupation, he would not only find inner peace, but would have closer ties with people who might be less racist.

After the necessary training, he was given the job as a priest in a local church. Louis began to live a more righteous life. And in the years to follow, he proved to be very helpful by giving counsel to hundreds of people about ways to become a better person.

* * *

A decade later, Louis began to experience a great deal of personal problems amid his life of celibacy. For a very long time he had been finding it difficult to control his physical urges, and now at this later stage of his life his sexual desire was getting stronger. Having been unmarried for such a long time, he had to constantly wrestle with his longing to have a relationship with a woman despite his respect for the rules of the church.

Unfortunately for Louis, after a decade of restraining himself from sexual intercourse, he decided one day to secretly visit a brothel twenty miles away. Louis believed that by having a secret relationship with a prostitute who was far away, he could still play an active role in the church without people knowing about his lapse. The prostitute Louis chose was a beautiful woman named Zebe. At this brothel, most of the other prostitutes disliked Zebe because she was considered the most beautiful, and attracted more men than the others. As this relationship between Zebe and Louis blossomed, Zebe no longer took an interest in other men and seemed contented to be with only Louis.

Many prostitutes advised him to stay away from Zebe, claiming that she had a terrible disease and was keeping it secret from him. Not wanting to question Zebe about this, Louis ignored them, believing that these women were only trying to discourage him because they were jealous of Zebe. Fortunately for Louis, since none of them knew about his past, much of the small talk about him and Zebe slowly faded away.

Louis' secret relationship away from the church lasted several months until a most unfavorable thing happened. One day when Louis came to visit Zebe, he learnt from another prostitute that she had contracted a serious disease and was in hospital. A concerned Louis hurriedly traveled to the hospital to see her, and he was taken aback when he saw Zebe's entire body covered with sores. Louis was reluctant to go very close to her, fearing that her disease might be contagious. While he stood aloof and pensive, Zebe was happy to see Louis as over the months she had grown to love him.

Seeing Zebe in such a sad state, one might have thought that

Louis would say something comforting to her. But instead he quietly told her to take some rest and he would come back the next day to spend more time with her. This promise never came true, for Louis abandoned her by hurriedly traveling back to the church and not returning.

Louis felt, since so far no one knew anything about his relationship with Zebe, and thinking she would probably die soon, it might be to his advantage to stay away from her. He was very afraid that the other prostitutes, knowing about the relationship he had with Zebe, might want to sympathize with him, causing more people to know about his involvement with Zebe.

At the hospital, Zebe in her illness remembered some of the happy moments she spent with Louis. For the short period she got to know him, she honestly felt that he was a caring person and that he would certainly come back to visit her.

Two weeks later, Louis woke up early one morning feeling very ill, and he noticed tiny boils on his hands and other parts of his body. Thinking that he might have contracted the same disease as Zebe, he decided to have himself checked at the same hospital as her. He chose this hospital because it was miles away from home so he could stay away from those who knew him well. Louis learned that he did have the same disease as Zebe, and he was instantly depressed, believing that he would soon die from this terrible disease.

Louis was admitted to the hospital and moved into the same room as Zebe, where a panel of doctors was closely monitoring their illness. While the medical staff worked diligently searching for clues as to the source of this disease, Louis in the meantime began to worry that his parishioners might soon find out that he was in hospital and would come to visit him.

One day while Louis and Zebe were alone, Louis made a

bold effort to get out of his bed to tell Zebe not to tell anyone about their secret affair. To win her affection, he told her how much he loved her, and that the reason he could not come to see her was that he had gotten ill the day after he had visited her in hospital. Though he was untruthful, he believed that by telling her this it might comfort her to believe that he really cared for her. A considerate Zebe, seeing the concerned look on Louis face, told him not to worry for she would keep their affair confidential.

Now that Louis was in a similar predicament as Zebe, he began to feel guilty for having abandoned her when he first discovered her illness. At this point, he deeply regretted neglecting her and was now willing to make amends.

Believing that they were going to die, Louis and Zebe began to reflect on some of the mistakes they had made in life and wished for something favorable to happen so that they could turn over a new page in life. Fortunately, days later when doctors began treating them with a new drug, the sores on their bodies began to slowly disappear. And within weeks of further treatment, they became completely cured. They were absolutely delighted and believed that they were given a second chance in life.

After they were released from hospital, Louis and Zebe began to meet more frequently to talk about changing their lives. In one of these meetings, Zebe told Louis that she was going to relinquish her livelihood as a prostitute. She then took a vow never again to have sexual intercourse with a man, and would from then on devote her entire life to serving the Lord. Louis seemed deeply concerned, for he recalled his earlier life of celibacy and how difficult it was to control his physical urges. However, upon reflection, he felt that this might not be too difficult for Zebe because she was choosing to abstain from sex based on a terrible experience and the desire to live a righteous life.

As Louis pondered on Zebe's decision, he felt that it was not necessary for him to now abstain entirely from sex, because he had already broke his priestly vow by having an affair with a prostitute. He came to think that marriage was a way to put an end to these feelings, and he was optimistic that doing so would help him to play an important role in family life.

After several weeks contemplating his future, Louis decided to relinquish his job as a priest. Many churchgoers became angry, claiming that he had gone astray. Amid all the criticism, Louis took the opportunity in church one day to confess his relationship with Zebe. Fortunately, when Louis explained to the congregation in a long and passionate speech how much difficulty he had controlling his physical urges, and the responsibility he took upon himself to live his life to please churchgoers, most of them were deeply touched and refrained from condemning him any further.

* * *

One year later, Louis fell in love and got married to a woman who later bore him two children. Life now seemed to have a greater meaning to Louis, for he not only enjoyed a good family relationship, but he found happiness when attending church with his wife and children. Though he deeply regretted some of the wrong things he did, he believed that God would not judge him unrighteous for renouncing his life of celibacy, but on the merit of his actions. To Louis, the life of celibacy he had lived earlier was not a rule of God that he had to follow, but a choice he had made to be in conformity with the rules of the church.

Acts of Terror

Gabriel Velasquez was once a shrewd diplomat who represented his country at the United Nations. As a clever mediator, he was greatly admired by other prominent officials for helping the UN in negotiations to avert war between nations, and on matters relating to food aid, human rights violations and environmental issues. Over the years his prime concern became unfair governments, which he felt were solely responsible for the suffering and hardships millions endure. On such issues, he was angered by the long-drawn-out discussions which the UN held, claiming that while the representatives of nations wrangled over problems, the sufferings of the poor got prolonged. As an outspoken person, he proposed many changes to the UN to deal with major problems relating to corrupt governments and acts of terrorism. But with the inadequate support he received, much of what he had to say was ignored, since some representatives were from nations ruled by dictators whom they could not condemn.

In Gabriel's eyes only the voices of the wealthy nations had the biggest say on matters relating to trade, territorial disputes and disarmament. And while they dominated all aspects of talks and negotiations, Gabriel observed that the representatives of poor nations were usually bored at meetings, listening to the prosperous nations wrangle over issues. To Gabriel, the majority of nations in the UN were not interested in solving the continuous problems corrupt leaders pose, since they were mainly interested in addressing issues that would benefit their own nation. Such concerns stemmed from his own observations that in places of unrest, some nations refrained from sending peacekeeping forces simply because there was nothing to gain from it, but instead left it to a strong nation or two to sustain order.

Gabriel felt that because of the selfish interest of some nations, it was extremely tough for representatives at the UN to agree on certain matters. In discussions on what he proposed, Gabriel discovered that many of them did not like his ideas, for they would not advocate punitive measures against corrupt governments because of the huge sums of money their government had invested in such nations.

When the representatives of some dictatorships tried to explain to Gabriel that their leader was not as bad as he thought, Gabriel got angry and rejected what they had to say. He could not accept their claim that a moderate dictator helps to sustain peace in a country where there are a number of radical factions, and where a sizeable portion of the population is aggressive and quick to advocate violence when they cannot get what they strongly desire.

For many years, Gabriel had been thinking of ways to lessen the problems of poor nations. With most nations being very much divided and reluctant to send peacekeeping forces to dismantle radical groups and overthrow dictators who had been suppressing millions for decades, he proposed that the UN create its own army to sustain peace and order. Such an army, he believed, should be under the command of the UN and made up of soldiers from every member nation. Gabriel felt that the lightly armed forces that some volunteer nations sent to sustain peace in troubled regions were no match for the sophisticated weaponry of some radical groups.

After a few years of being ignored by senior members of the

UN, Gabriel quit his job as his country's representative and became seditious. Taking the law into his own hands, he secretly began to gather up an army of volunteers from various corners of the globe who would embark on a mission to get rid of those he called tyrants. However, Gabriel's plans were leaked to the UN and he was strongly criticized by its members, who promised to do everything within their power to dismantle his organization. This made Gabriel angry, and he now became vindictive. Obsessed with his radical beliefs, he began working with his supporters to commit a series of terrorist acts against the UN.

During numerous bombings of administrative offices run by the UN, hundreds of innocent lives were lost. When Gabriel and his supporters heard through the media how seriously the UN was affected by these horrendous acts, they began to consider themselves heroes. However, as the taking of innocent lives worsened, millions around the globe began to view the members of this terrorist group as cowards, attacking mainly harmless people.

These horrifying acts on UN offices worldwide lasted many years, during which time Gabriel was proclaimed the world's most wanted man. His terrorist activities did not deter the UN and its member nations in their mission to find him. Many senior officials in the UN worried that if they did not get rid of Gabriel soon, he could easily become the problem leader of tomorrow.

From remote areas in the jungles of South America, Gabriel directed most of his terrorist activities abroad. Convoys carrying food under UN supervision to those in need were frequently attacked. Many nations, listening to Gabriel's threats, refrained from criticizing his group, fearing they would be attacked. This was very encouraging to Gabriel as it not only created a division within the UN, but also made him believe that he could possibly control such cowardly nations.

* * *

After six years as head of the Purple Guards Liberation Movement, Gabriel underwent a turbulent period of growing dissention within his group as to who should be the head of the organization. This rift was caused by the conflicting views they had regarding the planning of their terrorist acts. He had trouble controlling his followers, most of whom were uneducated and thinking of becoming leaders themselves. To add to his problems, he lost his wife one year after she had given birth to a baby girl. She was accidentally shot in the head by a stray bullet during his group's training for combat. After her death, Gabriel was left alone to raise his daughter Pandora in a harsh environment, for she was the only female among violent men.

During these years, young Pandora was slowly groomed to become a warrior. At a tender age she was taught how to shoot with a gun by her father, who felt a little insecure among men he was slowly coming to distrust. Gabriel felt that she could be a trusted bodyguard in the event that someone within the group tried to kill him. Before going to bed each night, he always left a loaded gun under a pillow that was within his daughter's reach. Being told by Gabriel to be watchful of anyone who might try to harm him, Pandora found it difficult to sleep soundly. Some nights when she could not sleep, she would sit on her bed admiring a beautiful painting of her mother that was hung on the wall. One night, in a gloomy state of mind Pandora decided to remove the painting. She became emotional and embraced it tightly, the sign of a lonely child who greatly missed that motherly affection. Just as she was about to put back the painting, she noticed that it was covering a small opening on the wall and inside it, she could see a small wooden box that was tightly sealed. From that night onward this small box became Pandora's favorite toy, for every night while her father lay sound asleep, she would quietly remove the box to play with it. And before falling asleep, she made it a habit to put it back so that her father would not be suspicious. After a while, Pandora became driven with desire to find out what was hidden inside the box. She made several attempts to open it but it was sealed tightly.

While Gabriel was asleep one night, Pandora quietly stepped out of their cave with the box held tightly in her hands, intending to see if she could open it with a hard object. As she looked around for some device to use, she saw a group of men sitting around a fire, quietly chatting. Seeing her from a distance, a man nicknamed Rico signaled to her to come over and join them. Surprisingly, Pandora smiled and began to walk slowly towards the group. Being pure at heart, she did not realize that some of these men disliked her father very much.

But then, Pandora suddenly stopped to think. It dawned on her that if her father should wake up and discover her missing, he might get angry. So, she turned and headed back towards the cave. Rico quickly approached Pandora and began to encourage her to join the group. Seeing her holding on tightly to the box, Rico asked her what was inside. When Pandora told him that she did not know, he began to plead with her to let him open it.

Rico, realizing that Pandora was determined not to open the box, suddenly grabbed it from her hands and tossed it high into the air. Unfortunately, the box landed in the middle of the fire, and the men laughed; however, as the box started to burn, there was a huge explosion which shook the earth. Within seconds everyone around the fire suffered a gruesome death, as their scorched and dismembered limbs were scattered in all directions.

It was clear that no one close to the fire knew that this box contained explosives, and what occurred came as a complete surprise. Only Pandora and Rico survived the blast with minor injuries, since they were far from the center of the explosion.

When Gabriel and other members ran out of their caves to see what had happened, they were in shock to find many of their associates killed. Amid all the excitement from the thunderous explosion, a terrified Pandora ran to and fro, screaming in fear. Gabriel hurriedly picked her up in his arms to comfort her.

When Pandora appeared a little more composed, Gabriel politely asked her to explain what had happened. In reply, she sobbed, "I do not know!" Gabriel told her that he was not going to harm her, but she must let him know if she had removed the box from behind the painting. Pandora then sobbingly replied, "Yes!" This made Gabriel certain that no one had come into the cave to remove the box. He then turned to Rico to inquire how the tragic incident had happened. To protect himself, he claimed that Pandora came out of her father's tent with a box and threw it into the fire, causing the explosion.

Young Pandora, still in a state of shock and confused by what had happened, did not deny what Rico said, so it was assumed that he was telling the truth. Other supporters who heard this felt that Gabriel must have had something to do with the tragic incident, believing that he must have filled the box with explosives and had given it to his daughter to throw into the fire to kill those he disliked. In fact, for many years this box of explosives had been a secret weapon of Gabriel, as he had plans to use it in the event that some of his disgruntled supporters decided to attack him.

From this tragedy, the members of this radical group became very worried, believing that Gabriel wanted to send a clear message that he was in control and willing to kill anyone who opposed him.

Over the next couple of days, Gabriel was very uncertain about the outcome of this matter, believing that some members might become vindictive and try to kill him. Instead, from this horrifying incident something favorable happened. Gabriel discovered that days after the tragedy no one opposed him. It seemed that the majority no longer had the courage to challenge his authority. Even Rico, who was partly to blame for what had happened, gave full support to Gabriel, fearing that if Gabriel found out his involvement in the incident, he might try to kill him.

Gabriel, now sensing renewed support, apologized to his supporters for the terrible tragedy his daughter had caused. He began to speak of unity and pleaded with his followers to remain loyal, for what had happened was not intentional, but an innocent mistake Pandora had made. Fortunately, Gabriel was able to convince most of his supporters, and the group was able to strengthen its resolve to continue their acts of terror.

In the days after the horrifying incident, Pandora became fearful of her father's associates, believing they might want to hurt her for causing the death of so many men. Her timidity was a serious concern to Gabriel, who was not one hundred percent sure about the loyalty of some of his supporters. He had this phobia that a disenchanted member might want to kill him while asleep or perhaps stab him in the back.

To restore Pandora's confidence, Gabriel began to instill hatred in her mind by telling her that he and his supporters were righteous men who were fighting against evil forces of the UN. Pandora being young and uneducated, it was not a difficult task for Gabriel to indoctrinate her with his revolutionary ideas. Being constantly told to hate those who did not believe in their cause, Pandora's confidence was slowly restored.

Several weeks later, in an effort to make young Pandora a full-fledged warrior, Gabriel and Rico brought a man who was accused of being an informant before Pandora and told her to kill him. Neither wanted this man to plead for his life so they ensured that his eyes and mouth were covered and his feet securely tied. As Pandora held the gun in her hand contemplating what to do, Gabriel and Rico encouraged her to perform this gruesome act. They lied to Pandora by repeatedly telling her that the captive was an unbeliever who opposed their cause, and that he had killed many of their supporters. Convinced that this man was evil, Pandora aimed and shot him several times. Gabriel and Rico were pleased, believing that she would forever remain loyal to them.

With supporters of this radical group now seemingly united, Gabriel, in an effort to motivate them further, started slowly to attach a religious element to his hortatory speeches. He began telling his supporters that what they were doing was righteous and sanctioned by the Almighty.

After months of this, Gabriel's supporters became more entrenched in his beliefs, and grew into a fanatical group which strongly believed that killing innocent people would help them to succeed in what they termed a righteous mission.

* * *

It was not until this terrorist group had claimed responsibility for killing a group of poor farmers, including innocent women and children, that public support grew for the UN to bring Gabriel and his supporters to justice. To the masses, he was viewed as a coward for attacking harmless people who dwelled at a subsistence level. Because of this strong public support, the UN through various covert operations was able to track down and dismantle the Purple Guards terrorist group. But the authorities were not one hundred percent pleased, as Gabriel and a couple of his senior supporters were not found.

Several months later it was learned from intelligence sources that Gabriel had secretly escaped to Mexico, but no one knew exactly where he was hiding. Although there was a great deal of speculation about his whereabouts, the years went by and Gabriel was never caught.

It was in Mexico, as the authorities had suspected, that Gabriel lived a quiet life in hiding with his daughter Pandora. Together they dwelled in a remote slum area, and looking rather ordinary, they fitted in quite well with their impecunious neighbors.

By this time, Gabriel looked much older, for he was now in his mid-sixties and bearded. In the ghetto, he appeared ordinary and peaceful, usually seen wearing an old unwashed jacket. To those who watched him stroll around the neighborhood, he appeared an elderly man who possessed little. However, hidden in the inner layer of his jacket, he carried thousands of dollars which he had accumulated over the years.

Dwelling in this isolated region, he was not able to spend his money freely, fearing that if he were to do so, his neighbors might become suspicious. Though Gabriel was old, he still had a compelling desire to commit one final act of terror and then escape to Bolivia, where he could dwell more comfortably and at ease. He was still bitter with the authorities for dismantling the terrorist organization which he had headed for almost a decade, and for imprisoning most of his followers.

Throughout Gabriel's dispute with the UN, his daughter Pandora was very supportive of his wrongdoings, since she was brainwashed by his revolutionary ideas. After years of quiet planning, Gabriel was all set to go ahead with his plans to escape to Bolivia, which were solely dependent on his daughter. However, just as he was about to put his plans into effect, Pandora gave him shocking news that she was pregnant by a man she had fallen in love with. She told her father not to worry, for he was a humble and compassionate person. Such noble qualities, however, did not impress Gabriel, as her unexpected pregnancy infuriated him. Seeing the disappointed look on her father's face, and fearing that he might want to harm the man she was in love with, Pandora decided to conceal his identity.

Pandora loved a poor farmer whom she got to know through frequent visits to his farm to buy fresh fruits and vegetables. During her pregnancy, she secretly visited her fiancée where she watched him and others till the land in the hot sun. While watching them work so assiduously, she developed a feeling of remorse and began to reflect on some of the horrible deeds she and fellow supporters had inflicted on innocent people. She was greatly saddened by the fact that she and her collaborators had once ambushed and killed a group of poor farmers to show the UN how determined they were if it did not give in to their demands. The more she reflected on this, the more she wept in guilt for all the wrong she had done. At times this puzzled her fiancée, who could not comprehend why Pandora would weep whenever she watched him till the land, and then leave suddenly to go home without revealing what was bothering her.

Soon, Gabriel became suspicious of his daughter's activities, for whenever she left the house to go shopping, he wondered if she was secretly visiting the man she loved.

Thinking about this tortured him mentally since he was very disappointed by Pandora's pregnancy.

One evening when Pandora returned home after visiting her fiancée, Gabriel confronted her as she entered the house, demanding that she help him with his plans to destroy an aircraft with its passengers after it landed in Bolivia. He claimed that in this plan only he and his daughter would survive.

When Pandora told him that she couldn't go along with his plans to commit this one final act of terror, his face reddened with anger. Such a menacing look was a clear sign that he had become stonehearted and unforgiving over the years.

Being old and a bit nervous, Gabriel realized that without Pandora's help, he could end up living a solitary life in Mexico, and not being able to spend the large amount of cash that he carried. A dejected Gabriel quietly walked into his room and sat on his bed pondering other means of escaping to Bolivia. Over the next couple of days, he was restless and bemused, since all the new plans he thought of required his daughter's help because he trusted her the most.

In the meantime, Pandora being pregnant and in love started to think differently, as life now seemed to have a different purpose. Thinking about the child she was bearing, she could not cope with the thought of collaborating with her father to kill the children of innocent people who would be onboard the aircraft. She began to plead with her father not to go ahead with his plans to destroy the aircraft with a bomb. This made Gabriel outraged and he punched Pandora in the face. As her nose bled profusely, he called her a coward and uttered the most profane language. Pandora sobbed, "You are a greater coward, only fit to kill harmless people."

These sensitive words aroused Gabriel's emotions, as he

briefly pondered on them. Seeing his daughter dazed from the blow, he reached out to assist her to get back on her feet. He then apologized to her for being so unkind. With pity he said, "I will not go ahead with my plans to destroy the aircraft, but all I ask of you is to help me escape to Bolivia." Pandora paused for a moment to think. It suddenly dawned on her that helping her father escape to Bolivia might be to her advantage, believing that as long as he lived in Mexico, he might want to harm the man she loved. So Pandora dried her tears and made a promise to get her father out of Mexico.

On the following day, Pandora got in touch with her father's trusted friend Rico, who was part of the terrorist organization in the past. She told him to come to their house as soon as possible, for her father had something of importance to discuss.

When Rico arrived at the house several hours later, Gabriel greeted him with a big hug. He was a tall muscular man in his late fifties who looked tough and in good shape. With a couple of deep scars on his right cheek and one over the eye, he gave the impression that he had been in a fight sometime ago. However, these were old scars he got when someone attempted to kill him by throwing a hand grenade into his car. He narrowly escaped because the assailant ran away thinking Rico was dead.

Gabriel and Rico were good friends for many years, and only became separated after their terrorist organization was dismantled by nations supporting the UN. For the greater part of this meeting, Gabriel had little to say as he allowed Pandora and Rico to make plans for him to travel to Bolivia using fake identification. Pandora suggested that she would travel first class with her father seated in a wheelchair, believing that this would be least suspicious.

After a lengthy discussion between Pandora and Rico, Gabriel insisted on taking his loyal friend Rico for a walk around the neighborhood. They were old pals who had a lot in common to talk about, since they had worked collectively on a number of terrorist acts in the past. As they ambled through the slum area, Gabriel told Rico the whole story about his daughter and how he no longer trusted her, as she had become too softhearted. He told Rico about his original plans to travel to Bolivia and then destroy the aircraft after it landed. Rico, being a heartless man, loved his idea.

Without Pandora's knowledge, they collectively worked out a plan for Rico to arrange with an airline employee to secretly hide a time bomb in the refreshment cart that is usually pushed along the corridor of an aircraft. This cart was to be made two-sectional, one part for storing food and the other packed with explosives. It was also arranged for the number two to be marked on both sides of it. Their plan was to have a bomb set to explode eleven minutes after the plane touched down. Since Gabriel would be making this flight as a disabled person, it was assumed that he would most likely be the first passenger to disembark, and by this time, the cart loaded with explosives would certainly be towards the back of the aircraft. Pandora had no idea about this secret plan and had one thing in mind, to simply take her father safely to Bolivia and then return to Mexico.

At the airport their plans went well and were not suspected. Pandora was seen as a pregnant woman pushing a wheelchair with an elderly person. Many flight attendants were considerate, for they assisted them with their baggage and allowed them to board the aircraft first.

On the aircraft, Pandora sat beside her father a few feet away from the front exit door. She helped him put on his seat belt, as he appeared too nervous to fasten it. Being a little apprehensive that something might go wrong, Gabriel was very unsettled as he frequently glanced at his watch, counting the number of minutes remaining before the plane took off.

Finally, the plane left the airport and Gabriel breathed a sigh of relief. He tilted his seat back and stretched his legs outward to be comfortable. He appeared much more relaxed and confident that he would reach his destination safely. After twenty minutes of flying time, one of the flight attendants wheeled the first refreshment cart along the corridor. As it got closer to Gabriel, his eyes opened wide, slowly turning his head to see if the number two was written on it, the number to confirm which cart contained the explosives. Unfortunately for Gabriel, the cart was unmarked. He then had to wait patiently for a second cart to come along, and on this occasion when it was wheeled along the corridor, he saw the number two clearly written on it. This convinced him that he was going to succeed in pulling off this horrible act.

For those onboard the aircraft it was a relatively smooth flight, and like most travelers, the majority seemed eager to get to their destination. As the plane began to make its descent, Gabriel looked at his watch and saw that the arrival time of the flight was going to be right on schedule. From that moment on, he glanced at his watch more frequently, since he realized that from the time the plane touched down, he only had eleven minutes to get off.

Pandora totally unaware of her father's plans, was in the meantime silently praying that the immigration authorities would not question them in detail. When the plane came to a final halt and passengers began gathering their hand luggage to disembark, Pandora told Gabriel that she was feeling nauseous and desperately needed to go to the toilet aboard the aircraft. Gabriel became nervous and instantly shouted "No!" But so many onlookers heard him yell that Gabriel felt embarrassed and told his daughter to go quickly. Pandora, totally unaware of the bomb, slowly eased her way through the passengers to get to the toilet. Gabriel in the meantime anxiously waited for the door to open so that he could get off. At this time one would imagine that Gabriel would also be concerned about Pandora's safety, but at this crucial moment he was selfish, thinking about his own survival. It appeared that fulfilling his evil desire was more important than saving his daughter's life.

Finally, the door opened and, because it was assumed that Gabriel was disabled, he was allowed to disembark first. A flight attendant, believing that he needed extra assistance, began to gently push the wheelchair that he sat on. She moved so slowly, he became agitated, thinking that it was only a matter of seconds before the bomb would explode. Suddenly, Gabriel jumped out of his seat and ran. As the flight attendant watched him in shock, the aircraft exploded, instantly killing the majority of passengers including Pandora. The sound of people screaming for help amid the horrifying blast created panic as people ran wildly to avoid the falling debris from the aircraft.

From the explosion, Gabriel received numerous cuts and bruises from the wreckage as the scattered fragments fell over a huge area. As the fire brigade, police and paramedics rushed towards the scene, Gabriel amid all the excitement got lucky, as he bypassed immigration and was rushed to hospital for treatment. It was there that one of the nurses observed that the old jacket Gabriel wore was ripped at the sides, and that there was money showing through. She quickly informed the police who immediately detained Gabriel. Later, under intense questioning, he was proven to have false identification. After a thorough investigation, Gabriel was discovered to be the terrorist who was responsible for the senseless killings of hundreds of innocent people.

Days later when Gabriel was brought to trial, hundreds of people stood outside the courthouse demanding that he be tortured and hanged. When he saw the angry mob calling for his death, he was frightened. Inside the courthouse, Gabriel surprised everyone when he pleaded guilty, and confessed that he was a coward who did not achieve anything from his acts of terror. In the end, when the verdict was handed down that he be sentenced to death by electrocution, Gabriel tearfully expressed deep regret for having taken the lives of so many innocent people.

How Attitudes Change

Mark Edison and Ted Fisher were two successful businessmen who grew up in Los Angeles. Through their assiduous efforts they became the owners of five popular hotels. Their friendship started in high school and because of their close affinity, they seemed inseparable. Both had similar interests and even got married on the same day to two charming young women.

At the end of each working day it was common for them to have a private meeting to discuss work-related issues. During one of these meetings, Mark told Ted that he had a sensitive issue to discuss with him, and hoped that they would not harbor ill feelings for each other. Mark confessed that for many years he had been suppressing his inner feelings by not telling anyone that he was strongly attracted to members of the same sex, and he was having an extramarital relationship with a wealthy businessman.

Ted, being a devout Christian, was taken aback by the news and for a brief moment there was complete silence in the room as he sat on his chair speechless. In private conversations with relatives, Ted had always spoken passionately against same–sex marriages, viewing them to be morally wrong. But hearing now that his best friend was homosexual, he had to rethink matters, since he did not want to say anything to offend his loyal friend. He decided to reason with Mark on the issue for he honestly felt that as mature men, they ought to discuss this sensitive issue discreetly. Ted was first to break the silence and began by saying, "How will your wife and children cope with the news that you are in love with someone of the same sex?" Mark explained that he was going to have a private talk with his wife to let her know how much he had suffered over the years by suppressing his inner feelings so as to maintain a good family relationship. Mark knew that such news would be heartbreaking for his wife, but he was willing to undergo this turbulence so that he could be closer to the man he loved.

Ted was inclined to think that Mark had been contemplating this for a long time, and now he seemed willing to go ahead with his personal plans. In an effort to get Mark to reconsider, Ted began to speak about the moral aspect of this issue. He pointed out that if young children were to grow up in a society where they are told that being gay is tolerable, then they are likely to choose between the sexes, and at such a tender age, children could easily be influenced to follow what many consider immoral. Ted believed that this could contaminate a society in that same-sex relationships might increase, and lead to total disrespect for those with moral concerns.

Mark responded that this was not a moral issue, as same-sex relationships had been around for centuries, and for decades many had been denied the right to love someone of the same sex. This, he believed was not fair, as many gays and lesbians had been treated unfairly and at times looked down upon with scorn.

Ted nodding his head asked, "If you should get married to this man you love, do you intend to raise children by adoption or even as your own?" Mark answered, "Yes!" claiming that homosexuals should have the same rights as heterosexual couples. In response, Ted pointed out that a child likes to grow up knowing that his mother is a woman and his father is a man. And that one has to consider how much a child could suffer if he or she is being taunted by others for having parents of the same sex.

As their conversation continued, Ted realized that Mark was not going to change his mind about this relationship. He then made it clear that Mark had a choice, either to remain the male head of his family or follow his inner feelings to be with his male partner. Mark explained that this was not a matter of choice, for his physical urges were different. From a tender age he wanted to do things that most girls did, but he had to contain these feelings, fearing his parents and friends would reject him. He honestly believed that there are thousands of young boys who probably have the same feelings as he has been experiencing and are probably afraid to talk about it. Ted demanded, "Why did you choose to get married and have children, knowing that you were attracted to others of the same sex?" This question appeared to puzzle Mark as he paused for a moment to think. He then explained the feelings he had then were mixed, that he had urges for both males and females. With everyone treating him like a normal male, he honestly felt it would be appropriate at that time to marry a woman. Mark went on to say that in his situation he was not born gay, for he was a boisterous boy who had lots of male friends. However, in his early teens his sexual preference periodically changed, making it difficult for him to choose between the sexes.

Though Ted was very much against same-sex marriages, he found it difficult to criticize his trusted friend, thinking about the predicament Mark was going to be in when his wife found out about his affair with another man. He told Mark that whatever decision he made, he would still remain a loyal friend. However, as a friendly piece of advice, he suggested that Mark should let the relationship between him and his same-sex partner remain private, for the more it became public, the more they would be disliked by those who believe that a sacred marriage is only between a man and a woman.

Several weeks later, Mark told his wife about the extramarital relationship he was having with another man and this shocking news greatly disturbed her. She got furious and told him that she would seek a divorce immediately. What she had to say was of little concern to Mark, as he had been preparing himself mentally for an insolent reply. However, when he saw how much his children were affected by the news of his relationship, he became worried. To the children it was the sudden end of a loving family relationship. Sadly, when their neighbors and friends learned why Mark and his wife were getting divorced, both children became the subject of gossip, and this turned out to be painful as they were taunted at times.

Mark and his wife separated and Mark moved in to live with his male partner. With Ted and Mark still maintaining their friendship, Ted was eventually introduced to Mark's same-sex partner whom he found amicable. From his disposition and the way he conducted himself among fellow businessmen, Ted could never imagine that he was homosexual.

One day at a social gathering for some popular businessmen, Ted overheard some of them talking to Mark and his same-sex partner about their relationship with other men, and about the need for them to seek certain rights and freedoms. Ted was stunned by this and thought that this clique of businessmen would have no problems getting what they desired, since they knew many prominent judges and members of parliament who could push through laws for more same-sex rights. Ted was a part of this elite group and did not realize until now what their sexual preferences were. He believed that this was kept secret from him because Mark knew how much he was against same-sex marriages. However, because many within this group assisted him in his business deals, he decided to maintain a good business relationship with them by accepting them for who they were.

Over the coming months, Ted began to mingle more frequently with men who seemed to love one another. It appeared to him that these men were not homosexuals as such, for they were married and had children of their own. He believed that they were bored with their wives and were probably seeking a relationship with a member of the same sex based on their feelings or the desire to try something different.

After weeks of being closely associated with this elite group of men, Ted got to like their camaraderie and began to socialize with them more often. Being treated with affection, he developed a special fondness for them. However, amid this male bonding, the most shocking thing happened: Ted fell in love with another man who was a close business associate. No one could ever have imagined that he had now become what he once despised. His friend Mark was happy when he heard about Ted's relationship. In the end, Ted divorced his wife and was happier being with men who seemed willing to exchange partners and attract others in promoting same-sex relationships.

The Sons of Ivan Hayley

It was a rainy night in the month of May when Ivan Hayley became seriously ill after developing a severe case of pneumonia. While it rained heavily outside, his four sons closely watched in despair at their father gasping for breath. As Ivan struggled to breathe, he kept clenching his fist tighter on a sealed envelope which he had been holding for hours. Looking pensively at him, his eldest son Luke was worried, that if his father died, he would have to shoulder the responsibility of raising his three teenage brothers.

For the sons of Ivan Hayley life was tough, for their mother had passed away only one year ago, leaving their father to raise them on a farm that was very isolated. Luke, the eldest, was Ivan's favorite son, for he was considered the most sincere and hardworking of them all. From a tender age Luke was fond of reading Bible stories, which seem to have contributed a great deal to his strong moral beliefs. And now, as he watched his father slowly dying, he began to read some comforting words from the holy book. While Luke prayed with sincere devotion, his brothers lowered their heads in a show of respect. Just as Luke finished the final prayer his father slowly released the envelope from his hand and quietly passed away. Ivan's youngest son Andrew seemed most affected by the loss of his father, since for the greater part of the night he wept in sorrow.

Luke now had the responsibility to take care of his three younger brothers, who had a great deal of respect for him.

However, days after their father's funeral, Luke's second brother Paul and the third one Daniel urged him to open the envelope which their father had left. Without hesitation, Luke gave Paul the envelope and told him to open it. Paul hurriedly opened it, and from the look on his face, the others could tell that he was greatly disappointed. Luke requested that Paul give him the letter to read. He discovered that his father had left his entire estate of twenty acres of farmland to him and nothing to the others. This was a huge disappointment for Paul and Daniel, believing that their father loved his eldest son the most and cared less about them. Luke considerately told his brothers not to worry, for they should consider the land as belonging to all four of them, and they could grow whatever crops they desired. This kind offer pleased his brothers, since they knew their eldest brother was always kind at heart.

Several weeks later, while tending to the crops, Luke saw his three brothers having a discussion with two men who came to visit the farm. Upon inquiring the reason for their visit, Luke learnt that they were making a deal with his brothers to grow coca plants on the farm. These strangers were talking about the huge profits they all could make from selling the coca leaves to make cocaine. Hearing about the thousands of dollars they could make by becoming part of a drug trafficking ring made his brothers very excited, and they pleaded with their elder brother to accept the offer.

Growing the coca plants for unlawful use was totally unacceptable to Luke, who had strong moral convictions and respect for the law. Unable to convince Luke to seize the opportunity to become wealthy, his younger brothers became very angry and asked him to leave the farm and go elsewhere to live. Luke was defiant, claiming that the land he inherited from his father would never be used to grow crops for illegal use.

In the days to follow, Luke found it difficult to get along with his brothers, as they were no longer friendly and refused to speak to him. However, in spite of being shunned, Luke made every possible effort to communicate with his brothers, pleading with them not to get involved in anything unlawful. With a great deal of concern, he explained to them the consequences of violating the law. But what he had to say was of little importance, since they felt that selling the coca leaves for illegal use was a way to extricate themselves from poverty.

One day when Luke returned home after tending to his crops, he was suddenly confronted by his brothers who held him at gunpoint. They demanded that he leave the farm immediately and seek elsewhere to live. This was a shocking surprise for Luke, as he could not comprehend how his brothers' outlook on life changed so quickly after the death of their father. Luke vehemently said that he would not leave, claiming that legally, he was the rightful owner of the land because he had inherited it all from his father. His brothers suddenly pounced on him and began to beat him. They then demanded again that he leave the farm and never return.

A badly beaten Luke began to walk along a lonely road wondering where to go. He was terribly ashamed of the dispute he had with his brothers, as they had always been considered peaceful and well-mannered. Since his brothers were teenagers, Luke did not want to get police involved in their family dispute, fearing they could be charged with an offence that might attach a stigma to their reputation.

Having walked for several miles, Luke came to a farmhouse that was owned by an elderly couple who knew his father very well. Seeing him badly bruised, the couple inquired about what had happened to him. To protect his family's reputation, he told them that he had a dispute with his brothers and he desperately needed a place to stay. Luke never mentioned to the couple that the dispute he had came as a result of his brothers wanting to get involved in drug trafficking. Seeing how distraught Luke was, the couple was sympathetic and offered him a place to stay. In return for their kindness, Luke promised that he would help tend to their crops and assist in their daily chores.

* * *

A year later, Luke decided to secretly visit the farm he owned to rekindle the relationship he had with his brothers. Arriving there, he was taken by surprise to see acres of coca plants being grown on most of it. This made him furious, believing that what his brothers were doing was wrong and in violation of the law. Without hesitating, he traveled to the city to inform the police about his brothers' involvement with cocaine.

At the police headquarters, Luke was told to wait for two policemen from a special task force who were called in to investigate the matter. After waiting patiently for over two hours, Luke was transported by the officers to the farm. As the officers drove up to the farmhouse, Luke was surprised to see his brothers coming out to greet them. This greatly disappointed him; he quickly realized that these officers were friends of his brothers and part of the same drug trafficking ring. The two corrupt policemen did not lay any charges, but simply told the four brothers to solve their own differences. Then the officers hurriedly left in their vehicle, leaving Luke totally stunned.

As soon as the officers were out of sight, Luke's brothers held him at gunpoint, tied his hands and feet and took him to the farmhouse where they locked him in a room. He was held captive and treated very much like a prisoner.

At the farmhouse, many who were part of this drug trafficking ring came to visit Luke's younger brothers to carry out their secret cocaine deals. Over the next few days, Luke overheard many of his brothers' conversations, for the room he was confined to was adjacent to theirs. He heard them talk about the large sums of money they were paid, and the need for them to purchase more guns to protect themselves against those who might try to cheat or harm them.

One day as Luke reflected on how deeply involved his brothers were in crime, he heard the voices of two men, claiming that they had caught someone who had been leaking information to the police about his brothers. This individual was being held at gunpoint and brought for questioning. As Luke quietly listened, he could hear them threatening to kill the accused if he did not tell them what he had reported to the police. Luke began to plead with his brothers not to harm this man. But this did not deter them, as Paul grew furious and threatened to kill Luke if he did not remain quiet. When the accused did not comply with their demand, his brothers began to beat him. Unable to gather any information from the man, Daniel became filled with anger and shot him in the chest. As the man lay on the ground gasping for breath, Paul who was also angry shot him a second time, instantly killing him. Their youngest brother Andrew, who was only fourteen years of age, became terrified and began to weep, for he had never seen anything so ghastly. His sobbing seem to indicate that he regretted getting involved in such serious crimes, and perhaps was too young to cope with this violent approach to life.

From this incident, Luke began to think that his brothers were a serious threat to society in that they were prepared to kill anyone who tried to stem the flow of their illegal activities.

Being held captive and not able to disapprove any wrong they did, he began considering means of escaping from the farm. Fortunately for Luke, this opportunity came one night when two of his brothers were away and had left their youngest brother Andrew to guard his room. Alone in the farmhouse, Luke began to plead with his younger brother to free him. He emphasized the strong brotherly love he had for Andrew, and urged him not to follow the footsteps of Paul and Daniel, or he would be killed one day. In an attempt to win Andrew's affection, he reminded Andrew how well he had treated him and his brothers over the years and about the good relationship they had as a family.

After listening to Luke's plea, Andrew expressed his concern, claiming that if he set him free, his brothers would certainly kill him. To make Andrew less apprehensive, Luke explained that he had tried everything to get Paul and Daniel to stop doing wrong, and should they try to hurt his youngest brother for setting him free, he would have no other choice but to fight them. Andrew knew that his eldest brother was a righteous person and doubted very much that Luke would harm anyone, so he turned Luke down. In one final plea, Luke claimed that if he were not allowed to escape, Paul or Daniel would kill him one day, and Andrew would live with guilt for not doing anything to help him. Andrew became sympathetic and decided to set free his elder brother. He gave Luke a loaded gun and told him to run away. Luke made a promise that if his brothers ever hurt Andrew for setting him free, he would kill both of them.

It was raining heavily outside and because it was only an hour before sunrise, Luke decided to hide amid the coca leaves in the pouring rain until Paul and Daniel returned to the farm. His intention was to lurk around to see how the brothers would react to hearing that he had escaped.

Early the next morning, Paul and Daniel arrived at the farm. Seeing them walking towards the farmhouse, Andrew quickly jumped into bed pretending to be asleep. When they saw him sleeping, they immediately awoke him. Usually at this time in the morning, they had breakfast before tending to their crops. After the three of them had eaten, Paul took whatever food was left to give to Luke, and upon doing so, he discovered him missing. He instantly became outraged and began accusing Andrew of allowing Luke to escape. Andrew, seeing how furious his brothers were, claimed that he had fallen asleep and had no idea how Luke had escaped.

Both Paul and Daniel became suspicious of Andrew, since they realized that with both of Luke's hands and feet securely tied, there was no possible way he could escape unless someone had assisted him. They both began to threaten Andrew by telling him that they would kill him if he did not speak the truth. Since he was reluctant to do so, they began to beat him. Though Andrew was harshly punished, he remained determined not to disclose any information about Luke. Unable to get any information from Andrew, Paul in anger pulled out a gun and shot him in the head.

Hearing the gunshot, Luke, still hiding amid the crops, knew that something had gone wrong and shouted at them not to harm Andrew. Paul and Daniel immediately ran outside eagerly looking around for Luke, but were unable to see him. An angry Paul shouted that he had killed Andrew and was now coming to kill him too.

Peeking through the coca leaves, Luke remained silent and monitored their movements. With the loss of Andrew, he was now determined to kill both Paul and Daniel. He felt that if he did not kill them, they might take many more innocent lives with their evil desires. Though he considered it an unrighteous thing to do, he felt he had enough justification to kill his brothers in what he considered a war against those who are corrupt and have absolutely no respect for the law. When Luke considered that his brothers were killers who had friends in the police force, he lost confidence in the justice system, believing that most likely they would be set free if caught. Because of the serious threat his brothers posed with their ongoing criminal acts, he felt that he could not "turn his cheek" and ignore them, otherwise evil would triumph.

As Luke hid in the field thinking about killing his brothers, Paul and Daniel began searching for him amid the coca plants from separate areas. As Daniel got close to Luke who was silently watching every move he made, Luke aimed his gun and shot him in the head. Paul who was some distance away opened fire, shooting wildly through the fields in hope of killing Luke. Having unleashed a number of bullets, he called on Luke to give himself up. When Luke did not respond to his call, he began to walk haphazardly through the field, smashing the coca plants with his feet to see where Luke was hiding. As he got closer, Luke suddenly crept up from behind and shot him. As Paul lay dying, he cried out to Luke to help him. At this point one might have thought Luke would have shown some form of compassion, but he no longer trusted Paul and considered him a menace to society.

Slowly, a dejected Luke walked back to the old farmhouse. As he sat down to contemplate about having taken the law into his own hands, he saw the same two policemen who had once handed him over to his brothers, coming towards the farm. As the officers got closer, they became suspicious, for the coca plants looked as though they were ravished. Onto the front porch of the farmhouse, the officers discovered the dead body of Luke's youngest brother. Through the open front door of the farmhouse, they saw Luke sitting in a chair totally dejected. He recounted the whole story leading up to the shootout with his brothers. These two policemen, who were heavily involved in the same drug trafficking ring with his brothers, handcuffed him and took him away to the central police headquarters. Luke was charged for the murder of his brothers, and being the lawful owner of the farmland, he was also charged for growing coca plants on his farm for illegal use. Knowing that he was dealing with a seemingly corrupt police force, Luke was convinced that no one would believe his story, so he began to prepare himself mentally to deal with the consequences of violating the law.

Several weeks later, Luke was put on trial; he was declared guilty and sentenced to life imprisonment. In prison one might have thought Luke would have fallen into a state of despair after having passed through such stressful experiences. However, while alone he began contemplating on his duties in life so as to gain some form of justification for his unlawful actions. He knew that in the eyes of those who did not know the truth about what started the dispute between him and his brothers, he might be classified as an evildoer for having killed them. However, given the serious problems he had encountered with his brothers, he felt that he had to act forcefully to put an end to their wrongdoings.

Luke believed that by doing battle with his unrighteous brothers, he had fulfilled his duty in life by opposing what was wrong and trying to stem the flow of injustice. Though he was disappointed with the outcome of his trial, he honestly felt that one should not lose faith in the justice system. Life appeared to be an ongoing battle between the forces of good and darkness, and a few corrupt policemen should not deter one from their duty in striving to maintain a world of peace and order.

Survival

Otieno Taibu was only eleven years old when he was brought hungry and naked to a refugee camp in East Africa to join thousands of starving people who were surround by an army of bandits. With his face partly covered with flies, Taibu sat quietly among hundreds of undernourished children, hoping to be given something to eat. He was very dejected after recently losing both of his parents in a gruesome massacre between two rival factions.

From early childhood, Taibu was poorly fed and as a result, he grew to be abnormally thin. Being uneducated and somewhat superstitious, he held on strongly to the primitive beliefs of his parents that starvation was a form of punishment, and the way to extricate himself from it would be to worship the spirits of his ancestors, who would protect and guide him to a place where there was lots to eat.

At the refugee camp, Taibu found it very disheartening to watch hungry people being yelled at and whipped when they clamored for food. Witnessing people dying each day, Taibu began to fear that if he did not escape from this place, he would surely die from starvation.

After harboring these thoughts for several days, Taibu decided late one evening to quietly sneak out of the compound and make his way into a dense nearby forest. This was bold, for the jungle was known to be a battle ground for rebel groups who had set numerous death traps along paths in the jungle.

Now alone in the forest, Taibu began to walk cautiously,

occasionally stopping to rub his hands and feet, as he was constantly attacked by mosquitoes and crawling insects. Though it was painful to be stung, he ignored much of the pain and kept on walking deeper into the jungle. For young Taibu there was no point turning back, fearing he might be killed or die from starvation.

After an hour wandering through the forest, he became hungry and tired. While looking around for anything to eat, he became very excited when he saw a deer standing only twelve feet away and giving birth. His mouth began to salivate, as he had not eaten meat in a very long time. With his eyes totally focused on the deer, his plan was to wait until the animal had given birth and then grab the fawn to eat it.

Finally, when the deer had finished giving birth, Taibu hurriedly chased the mother away and then grabbed the newborn by the neck. But the mother quickly returned and began to make a mournful sound. Afraid that the deer might attack him, Taibu immediately released the fawn and began chasing the mother through the bushes with a branch he broke from a tree. When the deer was out of sight, he hurried back to the place where the fawn was lying. As he cautiously approached the fawn with the intention of pouncing on the animal, he was taken by surprise to see a mouse nibbling at the body of the newborn. Without hesitating, Taibu grabbed the mouse and shoved it into his mouth. Being very hungry and longing for the taste of meat, he enjoyed this very much, as he licked his lips and fingers several times. Having eaten the mouse, he snatched the newborn to kill it, but just as he was about to twist the animal's neck, he was suddenly confronted by a young tiger. He instantly became terrified. With his heart palpitating, he dropped the fawn and made an impetuous dash along a narrow track in the forest to escape. Without looking back, Taibu ran speedily until he became totally exhausted. Now tired and very much out of breath, he decided to stop and rest under a tree.

Early the following morning, he was found sleeping by a group of armed men who woke him up and began questioning him about where he came from. Speaking the same dialect, he recounted his escape from the refugee camp. Fortunately, since he was naked and undernourished, they believed his story and decided to let him go. As Taibu was about to walk away, the chief nicknamed Dikobe politely asked him if he had seen a group of armed teenagers while he was in the forest. Taibu promptly replied, no. Sensing that it might be important, Taibu asked the chief if these teens were his friends. But Dikobe immediately cautioned Taibu that these youths were very dangerous. He pointed out that they were a rebellious lot who had refused to give up their weapons after a peace accord was reached between the government and the leader of their faction. Since then these youths had been robbing and killing people in small villages, and because of their horrendous crimes, he and his men were on a mission to kill them. Dikobe added that so far these teens had killed practically everyone who had tried to talk peace or negotiate a deal with them to give up their weapons, and it was clear to him that carrying a gun and terrorizing harmless people had given these youths a strong sense of power. Having said this, Dikobe pointed out to Taibu where he should walk in the forest to get to the city of Takumu where it was more peaceful.

Taibu's journey to the city of Takumu was long and tiresome. To stay alive, he drank muddy water and ate earthworms and the eggs of birds which he got by destroying their nests. Throughout this journey he was hopeful that the spirits of his ancestors would guide him to the place where there was lots of food.

Finally, after covering a distance of fifteen miles, he arrived on the outskirts of the city Takumu, which he found quite different from any other place he had ever seen. The area he arrived at happened to be a busy market place where thousands of people came to buy and sell their produce.

Between the market place and the forest was a huge dumpsite where vendors threw rotten meat, fruits and vegetables. Seeing so much to eat, Taibu was delighted, believing that the spirits had guided him to this place where there was plenty of food. Being very hungry, he began to eat whatever food he found. This place became Taibu's favorite place to visit, and each day he made it a habit to eat all he could and then return to the forest to rest.

Days later, some people observed what Taibu was doing and told him not to eat the rotten foods. Taibu was very confused, as he could not understand their dialect. Frustrated in trying to get him to understand that the food was bad for his health, they became angry and chased him away from the dumpsite. However, this did not deter Taibu, for on the following day he returned and began to eat the rotten fruits once more. Seeing this, an angry man grabbed him by the hand and gave him a sound spanking, and then cautioned him not to come back to the dumpsite. After this, Taibu never came out of the forest, fearing that people might harm him. Sadly, however, only two days later he became very ill and could not comprehend what was happening to him. He was suffering a slow death from food poisoning. As he lay helpless on a bed of grass, hundreds of flies and insects began to converge on his body. In a sorrowful mood, he concluded that he had gotten ill because he had forgotten to pay thanks to the spirits of his ancestors for all the food he had found. Amid his sorrows he was grateful for one thing, that he had found the place he had always dreamed of, for in his world of poverty life was all about eating to survive. With such thoughts in mind, young Taibu quietly passed away.

NOTES

NOTES